ANIMORPHS

The Extreme

K.A. Applegate

SCHOLASTIC

The author wishes to thank Jeffrey Zuehlke
for his help in preparing this manuscript.

For Michael and Jake

Scholastic Children's Books,
Commonwealth House, 1–19 New Oxford Street,
London WC1A 1NU, UK
a division of Scholastic Ltd
London ~ New York ~ Toronto ~ Sydney ~ Auckland
Mexico City ~ New Delhi ~ Hong Kong

First published in the USA by Scholastic Inc., 1999
First published in the UK by Scholastic Ltd, 2000

ISBN 0 439 01296 1

Printed by Cox & Wyman Ltd, Reading, Berks.

10 9 8 7 6 5 4 3 2 1

The Extreme

If I morph to fly a million more times, I will never get over the sheer grossness of it.

We wasted about half an hour hooking up together. Six flies with senses designed to find dog poop. Not easy, but we eventually assembled into a sort of hideous squadron.

We took off. A nervous, disgruntled, testy little squadron of flies on a mission to intercept the cruellest creature on Earth.

Just another fun day of being an Animorph.

Even the book morphs! Flip the pages and check it out!

Look for other ANIMORPHS titles
by K.A. Applegate:

1 The Invasion
2 The Visitor
3 The Encounter
4 The Message
5 The Predator
6 The Capture
7 The Stranger
8 The Alien
9 The Secret
10 The Android
11 The Forgotten
12 The Reaction
13 The Change
14 The Unknown
15 The Escape
16 The Warning
17 The Underground
18 The Decision
19 The Departure
20 The Discovery
21 The Threat
22 The Solution
23 The Pretender
24 The Suspicion

MEGAMORPHS
1 The Andalite's Gift
2 In the Time of Dinosaurs

the andalite chronicles

Chapter 1

My name is Marco.

I doubt we've ever met, but I'll bet you know somebody like me. Every class has a Marco. You know, the one who's the smartest, wittiest, most charming, coolest and the best-looking.

That's me.

I can't tell you my last name. I can't tell you where I live, either, or anything specific about me that might help certain people find me.

Believe me, I wish I could. Anonymity has its downside. Last week, for example, I wanted to run through the halls of my school screaming my name so everyone could hear. I wanted to hop on a cafeteria table and dance on somebody's crisps until a hall monitor came to drag

me away. I wanted to call an assembly so everyone could congratulate me.

I'd got a date.

And not just any date. A date with the most beautiful girl in our whole school. If not the whole world.

Marian.

Not only is Marian gorgeous, with long, black hair, deep, dark eyes and dimples that make me want to cry every time she smiles. She's also nearly as smart, charming and charismatic as I am.

You can see we're a perfect couple. The only flaw I can find in her is that she doesn't seem to think my jokes are very funny.

That, and her taste in music.

You want to know the coolest thing of all about this date? Marian asked *me* out. I didn't have to do a thing. We were just leaving our music appreciation class together when Marian said to me:

"Wow, Marco, you really seem to know a lot about classical music. And may I say, you are an unusually handsome, manly man. I want you, I want you now."

OK, that may be a slight exaggeration. But she definitely said the part about me knowing a lot about music.

"Either that, or I can scam teachers like no one else around," I said.

Actually, I know next to nothing about classical music. But my dad's got a huge collection of classical CDs. Sometimes he'll hog the TV, watching documentaries about Mozart and Beethoven and other wild-eyed guys.

"Well, I have tickets to Symphony Hall this Sunday afternoon," Marian said. "They're playing Beethoven's Third. It's my absolute favourite symphony. Do you want to come?"

"Well, I'm more of a fan of his thirty-third," I said, hoping I wouldn't pass out at her feet. Marian had just asked me out on a date!

Marian gave me a quizzical look. "His thirty-third? I don't get it. Were you making a joke?"

"Of course! It's a joke, hah HAH!" I said, sounding only slightly hysterical. "I love Beethoven's Third. It's just so. . ." I wasn't sure what to say. I'd never heard the thing before in my life. Marian looked at me eagerly, waiting for me to finish my sentence.

"It's just so. . ."

"Beautiful?" Marian suggested.

"Yes!" I replied. "That's a perfect word for it. Although I was leaning towards exquisite. Maybe even rapturous."

"Oh, yes!" Marian cried. "It's all those things! So will you come?"

"Sure," I squeaked.

"Wonderful." Marian opened one of her notebooks and scribbled in it. She tore the

sheet off and handed it to me. "Here's my number. Call me and we'll make plans."

"OK," I said, casually stuffing the sheet of paper into my pocket. I was going to have it framed as soon as I got home, but Marian didn't have to know that.

"This is going to be so much fun." Marian sighed. She smiled and her dimples made my heart skip half a dozen beats. Then she reached out with her beautiful hand and touched me on my arm. My whole body tingled.

Either I had a major crush, or the cafeteria had served tainted meat again.

"Talk to you," she said, walking away.

"Uh-huh," I grunted.

Now this sounds pretty cool, huh? I mean, what more could a guy want than to be asked out on a date by the most beautiful girl in his school, right? For any normal kid, living a normal life, this would be, like, the high point of his entire existence.

Unfortunately, I'm not a normal kid. And I definitely do not lead a normal life.

Sure, parts of it are normal. I go to school. Do homework when I feel like it. Eat dinner with my dad. Watch TV. Play video games with my best buddy, Jake, and kick his sorry butt.

But there's another part of my life that's anything but normal. In fact, it's so bizarre, so insane, so absolutely *out there* that I wouldn't believe it myself if I weren't living it.

You see, I'm sort of a superhero. No, not Batman, although that's a good guess, with that whole very cool, handsome billionaire Bruce Wayne thing. Not Spider-Man, either. But I do fly, stick to walls, and toss bad guys around like they're plastic action figures.

Superheroes use their special powers to save the world. And that's what my five friends and I are doing.

Saving the world. Not from clowns like Lex Luthor or the Joker. I wish our arch-enemies were as tame as a bunch of comic book supervillains.

Instead, Rachel, Cassie, Tobias the Bird-boy, the Andalite Ax, my best friend Jake and I are battling an entire race of aliens who are trying to conquer Earth.

The Yeerks.

For your sake, I hope you've never heard of them. Because almost the only people who do know about them are the ones who've become their slaves.

The Yeerk invasion is a secret. But it's happening.

Believe me, it's happening.

The Yeerks are slimy grey slugs that slip into your ear and wind themselves in and around every crevice of your brain. Once they've done

this, they own you. Control you. They've enslaved you.

You become something we call a Controller. Someone with no free will. You can't scream for help, because the Yeerk controls what words come out of your mouth. You can't run, because the Yeerk controls how far and how fast your feet move. And you can't resist when the Yeerk in your head starts to recruit your family and friends into enslavement. Because you're a slave yourself.

Pretty scary, huh? But maybe the scariest thing of all about this alien invasion is that you can't tell Controllers from normal people. They look normal. Talk normal. Act normal.

For all you know, your parents may be Controllers. Maybe even your cute, loveable grandmother has designs on subduing the planet.

So fighting this war — and it is a war — tends to make a guy kind of paranoid. You can't trust anybody.

That's why I didn't tell you my name. And that's why, ever since we took a shortcut through an abandoned construction site one night, life, which I always want to find funny, has been mostly grim.

It was in that construction site that we met the dying Andalite prince, Elfangor. It was there that he told us about the Yeerks. It was there that he gave us the nightmarish power to become any animal whose DNA we could acquire. Our one pitiful weapon.

Ever since then, I have not been able to look at another human being without suspicion. No one. Not even Marian.

And that's why, after experiencing those first few moments of joy after Marian asked me out, the suspicion began to seep into my brain. The gnawing little worm of doubt. What if she was one of *them*? What if sweet, perfect Marian, with those gorgeous dimples, was a Controller?

Sure, I might not mind being *Marian's* slave, but being a Yeerk's slave is a different story.

One date, I told myself. *Then, before we decide to go steady, I can check her out.*

Chapter 2

"So then what happened?" Cassie asked me in free period the day after what had come to be called The Big Date.

Free period was being held in the school gym this week. They'd closed our usual classroom. Something about asbestos and lawsuits.

So instead of studying silently for an hour, a bunch of kids were playing basketball and volleyball while the rest of us, me and Cassie included, sat around on the seats and talked. It was a big improvement.

"Well, after I failed in a bold attempt to escape during the interval, we went back in and the orchestra started to play. Again. And they played. And played. And I considered yelling 'Fire!' just to get out of the place. And when I woke up everybody was gone, including Marian."

Cassie laughed her gentle laugh. "Oh, well," she said, flipping idly through a veterinary medicine magazine she'd pulled out of a folder. "It sounds like it was for the best."

"What do you mean, it was for the best?" I cried. "It was a total disaster."

"Yes. But it doesn't sound like Marian's your type."

"But she's the most beautiful girl in the whole school," I replied. "How could she *not* be my type?" I gave Cassie the fish eye. "Wait a minute. Did you guys watch her?"

"We *are* your friends, Marco," she said apologetically. "We had no choice."

"You guys kept her under surveillance for the last three days?"

"Well, it was mostly Tobias and Ax, since they don't have school. Anyway, she's not one of *them*. She never went near a. . ." She lowered her voice to a whisper. ". . .Yeerk-pool entrance."

I wasn't sure how to react to that. Yeerks have to return to the hidden Yeerk pool every three days. Marian was OK. Now the question was: was this good news or bad news? I'd blown my big chance. Was it better or worse that she was a normal girl?

Something else bothered me. Jake had

asked Cassie to tell me this. Obviously. It was a good choice. Typical Jake. He knew that Rachel would just ridicule me. He knew that if he talked to me himself it would seem like he was meddling. But Cassie had the gentle touch. The diplomatic skill to let me know, without making me mad, that they had watched my temporary girlfriend behind my back.

Cassie was watching me, waiting for my reaction. And I was just loading up to deliver something scathing-yet-not-overly-cruel when a shadow fell over us. I looked up.

"Hey, Marco. Hey, Cassie. What's up?"

It was a kid my age. He was a little bit taller than I am — which, I'll admit, is how it is with most people. His warm, confident smile made you want to like him immediately.

But I knew better. See, this particular likeable-looking kid wasn't a kid, and his smile wasn't a smile. Erek didn't attend our school. Erek didn't attend the human race.

The kid standing in front of us wasn't entirely real. What Cassie and I and everyone else were looking at was a holographic projection. Underneath the projection was an android. An android that had been walking the earth for hundreds of thousands of years.

Erek and his other android friends are called Chee. They were the companions of an ancient race called the Pemalites. The Pemalites may have been the most advanced species ever to exist in the history of the universe. So advanced they forgot all about primitive stuff like wars and worry and sadness.

Unfortunately, the rest of the universe wasn't so elevated. An evil race called Howlers attacked the Pemalites and destroyed their home world. Some survivors fled to Earth, but before they escaped, their alien attackers infected them with a disease that eventually killed them all.

The Chee, being androids, weren't affected by the disease. To honour the spirits of their former companions and creators, they infused the essence of the Pemalites into the bodies of wolves.

Now you know why your dog is always in such a good mood.

And since the Pemalites created the Chee in their own image, the Chee are pretty friendly themselves. In fact, they're pacifists, sworn — and programmed — never to harm another soul.

Still, they hate the Yeerks and help us out whenever they can.

"Uh-oh," I said, still feeling a bit cranky over the possibility that Tobias had been watching Marian through her bedroom window.

And I *hadn't*.

"'Uh-oh'? Nice welcome," Erek said, sitting down between us. "Would you mind if we talk in private?"

"I repeat: uh-oh."

The air around us began to glow. The sounds of the gym — kids talking, the bouncing of the basketball, the squeak of trainers on the court — disappeared. We could see everything happening in the gym, but it was as if we were looking out from inside a clingfilm bubble.

"I have extended my holographic projection to include the three of us," Erek explained. The Erek we were looking at now was a steel-and-ivory android that looked an awful lot like a dog, maybe a greyhound, standing on his hind legs. "Everyone else in the gym sees and hears the three of us talking about last night's game."

"Well, if that's all you want to talk about, why all the secrecy?" I said brightly.

Erek smiled grimly. Not brightly. I felt the sense of another "uh-oh" growing inside me.

"What is it, Erek?" Cassie said.

"Our sources tell us the Yeerks have been trying to develop a way to broadcast Kandrona rays using human satellite technology," Erek told us. "They seem to have found some place on this planet isolated enough to allow them to erect a satellite station without interference. If they're successful, they could turn every back garden swimming pool in the world into a Yeerk pool."

I felt sick to my stomach. "That is definitely not good."

Kandrona rays are what the Yeerks consume. Their food. They absorb it when they're in the Yeerk pool. It's their Achilles heel. They need the rays to survive.

Every three days when Yeerks go down to the Yeerk pool, they slide out of their host's brain and take a Kandrona bath. Meanwhile, most of the hosts, the ones who don't want to be slaves, scream and cry and struggle and beg to be set free.

I've been to the Yeerk pool. It's a bad place.

We've imagined destroying the Yeerk pool. It would be a huge blow to the Yeerks. And we would if we could, but the place is about the size of a football stadium, with better defences than the White House, the Pentagon and Fort Knox put together. We just don't have the firepower.

"You know, Erek," I said, "nothing personal, but sometimes I'm not so sure I like you. You're nothing but trouble."

Erek grinned his steel-and-ivory dog grin. "Sure you're not just cranky over blowing The Big Date?"

I shot Cassie an outraged look.

She winced. "OK, so the Chee helped us out. It's not easy to watch someone for three days."

"Great. Is there anyone, anywhere who doesn't know that I crashed and burned on The Big Date?"

"She wasn't your type, anyway," Erek said. "She had taste in music."

"Oh, so you're a big Beethoven fan?"

Erek nodded his android head. "I was the maestro's valet for quite a few years. He was an awful person, but he made music my masters would have wept to hear."

Chapter 3

We met after school in Cassie's barn — aka the Wildlife Rehabilitation Clinic — to discuss the situation. Cassie's parents are vets. While her dad runs the clinic, her mum runs the vet staff at The Gardens, an amusement park and zoo. Cassie helps out at the clinic, giving suppositories to cranky skunks and stuff. And let's face it: a wildlife clinic definitely comes in handy when we need to acquire a new morph.

The get-together was like opening night of the local freak show. Four kids who regularly become fur balls. Erek, the ancient Android. Tobias, the red-tailed hawk, keeping a look-out from the rafters. Ax, the Andalite, in his human morph.

Ax's human morph is a combination of DNA

from me, Jake, Rachel and Cassie. Together we make one disturbingly beautiful person.

Ax is the only Andalite on Earth. In fact, he's Prince Elfangor's younger brother. Ax was in his human morph because, well, let me put it this way: Cassie's mum and dad are about the coolest parents you'll ever find, but if they were to walk in and find their daughter shooting the breeze with a blue-furred, half-humanoid, half-deerlike creature with a mean scorpion tail, no mouth and four eyes, including a pair that sat on swivelling stalks atop its head . . . they would definitely freak.

"Do you know any more details?" Rachel asked Erek.

Rachel is your basic psycho-babe. And I mean that in a nice way. She's a tall, willowy, supermodelesque blonde. You might think she was a shopaholic airhead — until you called her an airhead. Then, after she'd removed your left kidney, you'd realize your mistake.

Rachel's a great person to have on your side in a fight. The only problem I have with her is that she's always *looking* for a fight.

"Details? I'm afraid not," Erek replied. "We've infiltrated much of the Yeerk force, but we don't have access to everything."

"Nothing at all about the *location* of the facility?" Jake asked.

"No. Just that Visser Three will be visiting it

very soon. We do know this: we've discovered the location of the Visser's new feeding pasture. It's close enough for you to fly there in bird morph. A Bug fighter is going to pick him up there tomorrow afternoon to go off and inspect this site."

Jake got his "Jake look". The sort of weary, worried expression he gets when he's faced with some decision that may result in all of us ending up dead.

Jake, who is Rachel's cousin, is our sort-of leader. Not because he asked to be. It's probably because he'd never ask to be. You know — he's one of those tiresomely dutiful, levelheaded guys. If you met Jake, you'd understand why we turn to him. Call it charisma. Something about Jake commands respect.

Not from me, of course. He's been my best friend for ever. I was with him when he was nine and ate an entire pie for a bet and ended up throwing up blueberries for an hour.

Jake looked around at all of us. Not exactly asking for a vote, but obviously wanting to hear from us.

<So, no problem, right?> Tobias said. <We fly out to Visser's Three feeding place and when the Bug fighter arrives, we hitch a ride.>

"That appears to be our only option. Op. Shun. Shunn," Ax confirmed. Andalites don't have mouths. They communicate in thought-speak. So

whenever Ax does his human morph, he's fascinated by the sounds he makes.

By the way, he's the *only* one who's fascinated.

I held up my hand like I wanted to ask a question in class. "I'm not allowed to hitchhike. Especially not with evil alien parasites. My dad is very definite about that."

Jake managed a brief laugh. Rachel gave me her "what are you, a moron?" look.

"It doesn't sound like my idea of a good time, either," Cassie said. "But if it's true the Yeerks are building a system that will turn any body of water into a Yeerk pool, we have to do everything we can to stop them."

I groaned. I can usually count on Cassie to be rational.

"OK," I said. "I'll be there, but I promise to complain the entire time."

"Do we need to take a formal vote?" Jake asked.

"No way am I going to miss out on this," Rachel said.

Big surprise there.

"No, no, no votes," I said. "Jake decides. Then if it goes bad we can all blame him."

<I'm there,> Tobias said. <But aren't we overlooking a key detail?>

"What's that?" said Jake.

<I mean, it's not a problem for me. But you

guys can't just disappear for a few days. This place could be in, I don't know, Nepal for all we know.>

"Nepal?" I echoed.

"That is a bit of a problem," Jake said.

"Perhaps I can provide a solution," Erek replied.

I held up my hand again. "Is it OK if I say 'uh-oh' again?"

Chapter 4

<Man, I just know I'm going to come back to a cupboard full of soggy comics,> I said. <I can tell by the look in Erek's eyes he's a bathtub reader.>

Erek's solution had been to have himself and three of his Chee friends program their holograms to look like each of us. Little did my dad know that he'd be sharing his cornflakes with an android who'd been on Earth since before the first flake was created.

It was the next morning and we were all in our various bird-of-prey morphs — Tobias as red-tailed hawk, Jake in his peregrine falcon morph, Rachel in bald eagle morph, Cassie and me in our osprey morphs and Ax in his northern harrier morph — flying towards certain doom.

Again.

We were on our way to Visser Three's newest secret feeding pasture. Erek had given us directions and wished us luck. "Good luck taking on the most dangerous creature in the galaxy. I've got to go and oil my elbow joints. Let me know if you survive, we'll get together, do lunch. Ciao."

OK, maybe that's not exactly what he said. But it's OK to resent a person who's going to be safe while you're going to be screaming and running for your life. Don't you think?

I've mentioned that I complain occasionally. Or constantly. Sorry, but any smart person knows there's plenty to complain about in life. And there are definitely a lot of things to complain about when it comes to being an Animorph.

However, flying is not one of them.

I mean, talk about fun! Talk about freedom! It's everything you've imagined and more.

We were following a highway out of town towards the forest that surrounded some nearby mountains. It was an absolutely perfect day for flying — sunny, warm, and so clear you could see for kilometres. The surface of the highway absorbed the sun's warmth, creating some really nice thermals, which are pockets of rising warm air.

We were spread pretty far apart. In the

animal kingdom, birds of prey just don't hang together. Each of us took turns flying over the highway, catching a thermal and letting it lift us in the air like an invisible elevator. Then we'd coast for a while, slowly drifting downward in the direction we wanted to go. We hardly had to flap our wings at all.

<Hey, guys, I think I found it,> Tobias called out. <See that clearing in the middle of those trees?>

I scanned my super osprey eyes ahead, towards the line of trees a kilometre off the road. Sure enough, just beyond was a big meadow, maybe about two blocks wide. And galloping around in that meadow was a blue-furred, four-eyed, scorpion-tailed Andalite. He looked like he could have been Ax's father.

He wasn't. He was the leader of the Yeerk invasion of Earth. The only Yeerk ever to have got control of an Andalite body — and of the Andalite morphing technology. The only Yeerk who can morph.

Visser Three.

Remember I told you about Ax's brother, Elfangor? The Andalite who gave us our powers? Well, the Visser didn't just murder him.

He ate him.

Visser Three morphed into some bizarre, giant alien and chomped him down like a piece of sushi. I saw it happen. We all did.

Now you know why I have an incredible urge to pee on myself whenever we come near this guy.

The Visser wasn't alone in his meadow. Despite his fearsome power, the Visser is never without a few bodyguards. We counted half a dozen human-Controllers disguised as state cops. And in the tree line lurked a pair of Hork-Bajir, the bladed shock troops of the Yeerk Empire.

<OK,> Jake said. <Each of us is going to land in those trees, one at a time at least three hundred metres apart, in at least five-minute intervals. Rachel, you go first, then Cassie. Each of you keep an eye on those who land after you, so you can find them as easily as possible once you remorph. Tobias, you're last. Stay up top and keep a look-out until we've all landed.>

<Let's do it,> said Rachel.

I sighed. <The three words I hate most.>

Chapter 5

I spilled the air from my wings and slipped through the trees. I landed silently on the ground, my laser-focus eyes locked on Visser Three all the way. If he showed any signs of noticing any one of us landing, we were going to take off without a second thought. That was the plan.

The Visser trotted through the grass, feeding through his hooves like any ordinary Andalite would do. The Hork-Bajir and human-Controllers looked outward, like Secret Service agents around the President.

I watched him closely to see if he noticed as we came in for our staggered landings. Nothing unusual. No sign his guards had seen us.

I flitted through the tree branches. Stopping,

flying, stopping again. Till I was just thirty metres or so from the Visser. Then I dropped to the ground, found cover behind a huge elm tree, and began to demorph.

Even though I've done it dozens of times now, morphing never fails to freak me out. I mean, talk about unnatural. It doesn't hurt, but it's still just creepy.

An itchiness washed over me as my feathers turned soft and ran together, transforming themselves back into skin. My wings, now pale flesh like a plucked chicken's, began to shrink and disappear into my shoulder blades. I could feel the bones in my legs creaking as they stretched out to their normal length and grew heavy.

SPLOOT! Suddenly, fingers. I could feel them twitching, but they were attached to my shoulders! Ugh. My arms sprouted out of my torso like plants growing out of the ground in time-lapse photography, pushing the fingers and hands out before them, reaching their usual length in a few seconds.

I was fully human now, dressed in ugly black cycling shorts and a tight, white T-shirt. We've never figured out how to morph clothes, other than skintight stuff. Forget shoes. It's probably not even possible. Andalites invented morphing technology. And since they don't wear clothes, morphing "artificial skin", as Ax says, isn't an issue for them.

I crouched there in the dirt for a few minutes, catching my breath before morphing again. This morph was nowhere near as fun as an osprey. In fact, it was downright gross.

I concentrated. I envisioned myself as a fly.

SCHLOOP! My arms and legs shrivelled back into my body with a sound like the one you make when you suck spaghetti into your mouth. Good thing I was crouching when I'd started or I'd have crashed to the ground.

Very annoying. No legs or arms. Unfortunately, every morph is different every time. You never know exactly how things will happen.

Then I began to shrink. The trees round me became taller and taller as I became tinier and tinier. The leaves on the ground next to me looked as big as car parks. I was fly-size now, but my body was still more human than insect.

I was not an attractive creature right then. Marian would not have asked me out.

My limbless torso began to divide itself into three parts. Six tiny, hairy legs shot out of my sides. An itchy spot on my back suddenly sprouted tiny gossamer wings.

All that remained of the morph was the part I dreaded most. Suddenly my two eyes began to pop. The two eyes became four. Then sixteen. Then two hundred and fifty-six. And so on. I saw the world through thousands of tiny, fuzzy TV screens, facing in all directions. Compound eyes.

A long tube sprouted out of my face, a proboscis that flies use to cover their rotting food with saliva before they chow down.

If I morph to fly a million more times, I will never get over the sheer grossness of it.

We wasted about half an hour hooking up together. Six flies with senses designed to find dog poop. Not easy, but we eventually assembled into a sort of hideous squadron.

We took off. A nervous, disgruntled, testy little squadron of flies on a mission to intercept the cruellest creature on Earth.

Just another fun day of being an Animorph.

Chapter 6

<How long until the Visser's flight arrives?> Jake asked Ax.

<Five of your minutes,> Ax said. One of the many nice things about having Ax around is that he has a sort of built-in clock that allows him to keep track of the time.

On the other hand. . . <Ax, I really think you can just deal with the fact that they aren't *our* minutes. They are everyone's minutes.>

Ax ignored me.

<Let's get this over with,> Rachel replied.

<OK,> Jake said. <Remember, if anything goes wrong, don't look back. Get out of there as fast as you can. Ax? What's the best way to sneak up on an Andalite?>

<From beneath.>

<OK, you heard him,> Jake said. <We buzz the grass, try to intersect him, come up beneath him, grab some Andalite stomach fur. Any questions?>

<Nah, why would there be questions?> I said. <I mean, it's all so simple and easy and normal. What could possibly go wrong?>

<Was that an example of human sarcasm?> Ax asked.

<Ax, it's sarcasm for anyone, not just for humans.>

<OK, let's get this over with,> Tobias grumbled. <Lousy fly eyes. I hate this.>

We kept low, down where a fly likes to fly. Down low where it can smell the rotting food and the animal faeces and other wonderful, tasty things.

We skimmed the wild grass tops. It was like flying at treetop level except that these trees were impossibly tall, willowy stalks that bent with every chance breeze.

We buzzed our crazy fly wings and bobbled and weaved and wallowed towards a vague blob of blue fur and bad attitude. Visser Three was still running, but slowing down. He was moving at an angle from us. We'd intersect in a very few minutes. Less, if he. . .

Turned!

<Yah! There he is!> Cassie yelped. <Quick, or we lose him!>

I cut a wild turn. A pair of flies zipped in front of me. Impossible to tell who. The chase was on!

Galumph, galumph, galumph. The Visser trotted, pursued by six panicked flies.

<Stay low!> Jake reminded us. <Go for the belly!>

A wall of blue fur galloped right across my line of flight. I saw two flies zip down and under the heaving curve and disappear from my limited sight. Then two more flies from out of nowhere.

My turn.

I shot through the air. Visser Three loomed straight ahead but I couldn't see clearly enough to tell whether his stalk eyes were looking in my direction. I focused on his stomach and made a beeline for it.

Fifteen centimetres away! I did the fly somersault, a mid-air gymnast kind of thing that brought me legs up and wings down, vectoring in like a wobbly rocket.

Five centimetres to touchdown! NO! He cut a sharp right and veered away.

I shot towards him again, but now he bolted to the left. <What's with him, is he drunk?> I demanded in outrage.

<Aren't you on board, Marco? Everyone else is here,> Jake said.

<No, we're playing catch. Ahh!>

He'd stopped suddenly. A hand the size of Colorado reached round, trying to grab me! I slammed into reverse, spun in mid-air, and zipped away. Only then did I realize the true target of Visser Three's hand.

He was scratching his butt.

<Marco?> A thought-spoken whisper. Jake. <Are you here?>

Suddenly, it got very dark.

A big black shadow, blocking out the sun. Something straight out of a science fiction movie.

A Bug fighter. They're called that for a reason. They look like a big, black cockroach. A roach the size of a school bus, with two long pincerlike things sticking straight out, like antennae with heavy starch.

The Bug fighter slowly lowered until it touched the ground. I froze. Visser Three froze. A doorway — or at least a rectangle of relative darkness — appeared in its side.

The big blue blob in front of me trotted inside.

I followed him.

Inside it was dark. A few lines of light along what was probably the ceiling and floor. An occasional box of light, probably display monitors. The air pressure around me suddenly changed as the entrance closed. I maintained and kept my eyes on the Visser.

<Marco? Are you here?> Jake asked again.

<Attempting rendezvous now, Houston. Ten seconds to contact.>

Visser Three came to a halt. I dived for his underbelly. Just as I felt his fur under my feelers, my brain exploded with the sound of very loud thought-speak.

<Is the Blade ship ready?>

Visser Three never whispers.

Something answered. A Taxxon? They're smarter than Hork-Bajir. Weirder, too. They eat their own kind.

But I couldn't see anything but giant blue stalks of fur. On the floor of this jungle was warm, pinkish-khaki skin. I didn't want to touch that skin. I grabbed a few blue stalks and clung.

<Ax, what was that Taxxon saying?> Jake asked.

<I believe he was stating estimated departure and arrival times.>

<And?> Jake asked.

<And I am afraid we have a problem, Prince Jake,> Ax said.

My fly stomach bounced. Then it bounced again. I clung tighter to the Visser's fur. We were taking off and I was fighting the fly's panic reaction: things vibrating means MOVE!

<What's the problem, Ax?> Jake asked.

<I am afraid our journey is going to be a long one.>

<How long?> I asked.

<Approximately three and a half of your Earth hours.>

<Uh-oh,> I heard Cassie reply.

<Oh, man!> Tobias said.

<You're kidding me,> Rachel said.

The reason we weren't happy to hear this news, of course, is that it meant we were going to have to demorph at some point in flight. Somewhere aboard a ship occupied by Taxxons and Hork-Bajir *and* Visser Three.

Chapter 7

<Three and a half of our hours! Where are we going, the moon?> Tobias asked.

<Don't *you* start with the our-hour-your-hour thing, Tobias,> I warned.

<No,> Ax replied. <Going to the moon would take less than three and a half of *your* hours. Our journey will take longer because we will be flying through the planet's atmosphere.>

<Any idea of our destination?> Jake asked.

<The navigator did not say. I will, however, do my best to gauge our direction as we go along.>

<Ax, you'd have made a great Cub Scout.>

<A what?>

<What are we going to do?> Cassie asked.

Good question. We were trapped on a Bug

fighter with our worst enemy. And now we had the choice of revealing our presence — suicidal — or spending the rest of our lives as rubbish-eating insects.

BOOOOM!

<What was that?!> Rachel cried. <Man, this fly does not want to sit still.>

<I think we are docking with the Blade ship,> Ax replied.

If a Bug fighter is like a bus, a Blade ship is like a jumbo jet. It's shaped like a battle-axe from the Middle Ages. And it's Visser Three's personal ship.

<This might actually be a good thing,> Jake said. <At least the Blade ship is big enough so we might find someplace to hide and demorph. No way we could demorph on the Bug fighter without being seen.>

<Have I mentioned that I hate this morph?> Tobias added. <I mean, I'm finding myself very attracted to the Visser's sweat. How sick is that?>

<Yeah,> Cassie agreed. <He stinks. But to my fly brain, he actually smells kind of good.>

<He certainly does *not* stink,> Ax said defensively. <This is an Andalite body, and Andalites have never been known to stink.>

Suddenly the air pressure changed, ever so slightly. Just enough to make me lose control. I started to fly, then cancelled that order and

ended up zooming back hard into the Visser's belly.

<Oops,> I said.

<Oops what?> Jake said tensely.

<Oops, he may have felt that.> I glued my wings down and managed to calm the jumpy fly brain just as six gigantic blue columns crashed down around me, digging across the skin and through the fur like massive ploughs.

<Oh, man, I'm being scratched!> I cried.

<Cursed parasites!> Visser Three shouted.

<Hey, he's one to talk,> Rachel said.

<Heads up, everybody,> Jake said. <Be ready to jump at any second!>

The first scratch missed me. As I tried to avoid the Visser's searching fingers, I jumped from palm-tree-sized hair to palm-tree-sized hair with blazing speed, like Tarzan after a gallon of Mountain Dew.

<Marco, stay still!> Jake shouted.

<That's easy for you to say!> I shouted back.

Suddenly the fingers stopped raking and formed a cage around me. Trapped!

<I'm about to get pinched!>

<Marco!> Cassie cried.

I felt a slight breeze wash over me. The kind of minuscule air movement only a fly notices. Then I felt a new vibration. Dozens of tiny impacts: the needle-sharp legs of a Taxxon.

<He's welcoming the Visser back aboard the

Blade ship,> Ax translated. <Or he may be telling him his brother is a meteor fragment. I understand *Galard*, but this morph's hearing is very uncertain.>

The Visser took his hand from his belly. The telephone-pole fingers withdrew.

<Are all the Venber on board?> Visser Three growled.

<Venber?> Ax asked excitedly. <He did say Venber, did he not?>

<I don't know,> Jake replied. <Is that important?>

<Hey, Ax. You're not holding out on us, are you?>

<I must have misunderstood,> Ax said, not exactly answering my question.

<Excellent,> the Visser replied. <With twice as many Venber, our project will be completed in half the time.>

<Well, at least he knows his maths,> Tobias said wryly.

And that was it for the better part of an hour. They say combat is ninety-nine per cent waiting around and one per cent sheer terror. They're right. We hung out upside down, clinging to Visser Three's stomach hair, and tried not to let ourselves be overcome by the unholy, screaming willies.

I mean, it's one thing being a fly when you're busy. But just hanging out, you start to notice

the spit dribbling off the end of your proboscis. And that's not good.

<So,> I said, <did anyone bring a deck of cards? Anyone seen a good movie lately? Anyone have any juicy confessions they'd like to make?>

We were in what must have been the Visser's private quarters. A spare room with no furniture except for a computer console. After all, he was in an Andalite body, and Andalites don't sit.

There were various things hanging from the walls, like art. Some were large and elaborate, made of steel or something like steel. Some had electrical probes. Some had teeth or spikes or saws. We had an idea they might be instruments of torture collected from around the galaxy.

We had that idea because I recognized one of the artworks: it's called an "iron maiden". Not the dinosaur rock band, the Middle-Ages cage with the spikes inside.

It was a little depressing to realize that some Earth museum had unwillingly made a contribution on behalf of Homo sapiens.

And it was even more depressing realizing that we were going up against a guy who thought you should hang an iron maiden on the wall instead of a *Baywatch* poster.

Chapter 8

We'd cleverly come up with two plans. Plan A involved Visser Three leaving the room voluntarily while the rest of us stayed behind and did a quick demorph followed by a remorph. But as time passed and the Visser made no move to leave, it looked more and more like we were going to have to implement the much riskier Plan B.

Fine by me. I was ready to do something or go insane. Inactivity makes for way too much time to think about things like death and destruction and pain and violence. Inactivity makes for fear.

Another good defence against fear is humour. From my point of view, if you're not laughing, you're crying. Humour as coping mechanism.

Besides, I sort of consider it my job to keep us loose in these situations. Entertain the troops.

<Say, Rachel, I got a joke for you,> I said.

<No you don't,> she said.

I ignored the warning. <Two blondes are standing across the river from one another. . .>

<Hey,> Tobias interrupted. <Remember, I'm a blond, too. It may be dirty-blond, but it's blond.>

<Yeah, for a couple of hours a week,> I said. <Anyway, the one blonde calls out to the other blond, "How do I get to the other side?">

<That is very funny, Marco,> Ax said brightly.

<I haven't told the punch-line yet, Ax,> I replied. <And the blond across the river calls back to her, "You ARE on the other side!">

<That does it,> Rachel said. <Time for Plan B.>

<I've heard that one before,> Tobias said, unimpressed.

<I am afraid I do not understand,> Ax replied.

<Tobias, where exactly did you hear that joke before?> I demanded. <A sparrow, an owl and you, hanging out and swapping stories?>

<Ax, do you have any idea where we are?> Jake asked.

<I believe we are heading north.>

<Still north?> Jake replied. <How much longer until we have to demorph?>

<About twenty minutes,> Ax replied. <Of *your* minutes,> he added, with what I swear was deliberate provocation.

<Good. Plan B. Let's do something, anything.> Rachel. Of course.

<Yeah. Suppose we should,> Jake said without much enthusiasm. <Ax, are you ready?>

<I believe so, Prince Jake.>

<Break a leg, Ax-man,> I said.

<Whose leg?>

<It's just a . . . never mind.>

Everything was quiet for a few seconds. Then our brains were bombarded with the sound of very loud thought-speak.

<Guard! Come in here immediately!> Ax bellowed. A pretty decent imitation of Visser Three.

I sensed a breeze filled with the scent of a Hork-Bajir warrior.

Visser Three's sudden, startled movement felt like a massive earthquake. I clung tightly to my chosen hairs.

<What are you doing, fool?!> Visser Three shouted at the Hork-Bajir. <What is the meaning of this interruption?!>

The Hork-Bajir muttered.

<Get out!> the Visser raged. <Get out or I'll feed you to the Taxxons!>

The guard left.

<Again, Ax,> Jake said.

Ax bellowed.

Another breeze. I smelled a different Hork-Bajir. I could feel Visser Three quaking with rage.

<What?!> he screamed. It was like being in a front row seat at a Beastie Boys concert. Right by the big speakers. I thought my head was going to explode.

A sudden muscle spasm. I knew right then that the Visser had snapped his deadly tail. Seconds later. . .

WHUMPF!

Something big hit the floor. I didn't want to think about what it was. Who it was.

<Once more ought to do it, Ax,> Jake said. I could sense his hesitation.

I almost felt sorry for the Hork-Bajir. They're just helpless slaves of the Yeerks. Whatever they do is at the command of the evil Yeerks in their brains. In fact, before the Yeerks conquered them, the Hork-Bajir were a peaceful race. They're just big, dumb, bark-eating lizards. And kind of sweet, really.

Innocent victims in a war that didn't seem to have any other kind.

Ax shouted a third time and I whiffed two Hork-Bajir entering. I suppose they thought two at once would help.

It didn't.

The Visser lunged, out of control with rage.

Towards the two Hork-Bajir, towards the door. Out!

<Everybody off!> Jake yelled. <Stay low!>

I let go and shot through the air. I watched as the huge blue blob disappeared through the doorway. The door shut behind him.

<Demorph and remorph as fast as you can!> Jake instructed.

I landed on the floor and immediately began to demorph.

Morphing's never logical. It never happens the same way twice.

This time, the first thing that changed were my eyes. Thousands of them went POP. Just like that, I had my human eyes again.

This was not necessarily a good thing, since it gave me the chance to watch everybody — including myself — demorph. And it gave me a really good view of the poor Hork-Bajir on the floor. At least he was in one piece. He might still live. Hork-Bajir are a sturdy bunch. Yeah, he might live.

If the Taxxons didn't find him first.

Chapter 9

Rachel's change was especially weird. At first, she just grew. Before my eyes she went from being a little speck to a hundred-and-fifty-centimetre-tall, thousand-eyeballed insect, with blonde hair sprouting from the back of her head.

Cassie has a talent for morphing. She does it better than any of us, even Ax. In a few seconds, she looked totally normal — except for the two gossamer wings attached to her back. She looked like an angel or a fairy godmother.

I looked at my hands. They were hairy claws, gigantic versions of a fly's leg. I watched as the thick hairs disappeared, replaced by my own body hair. The ends of the claws cracked open like eggshells. My fingers slowly slithered out, like five baby snakes emerging from their shells.

"Everybody take about two deep breaths and remorph," Jake whispered when we were all completely demorphed. Four humans, one red-tailed hawk, and one young Andalite.

Easier said than done. Morphing is like running a two-hundred-metre dash at top speed. You're not ready to collapse afterwards, but you're not ready to do it again right away, either.

I took a few deep breaths and concentrated on becoming a fly. I imagined those thousand eyes and those hairy legs. That disgusting proboscis.

Jake was already changing, getting smaller and smaller. Rachel's arms began to shrink and grow black hairs. Cassie's wings were sprouting. Tobias's intense hawk eyes began to double, triple, quadruple, while his hooked beak grew outward, transforming itself into a tube.

Ax and I seemed to be behind everybody else. Then we heard a faint hissing. We exchanged worried glances before turning our eyes towards the door.

The door slid open.

The unconscious Hork-Bajir's luck had just run out.

Taxxon! A tree-trunk-thick centipede with needle legs and weak claws and a red-rimmed mouth and raspberry-jelly eyes.

It saw me, only half-morphed. It was puzzled.

Then it saw Ax. An Andalite. No longer puzzled. Terrified! The Taxxon hasn't been born who can confront an Andalite.

<Ax!> Jake shouted. <Pretend you're Visser Three!>

<What is the meaning of this interruption?!> Ax shouted.

The Taxxon didn't reply. He wasn't fooled. He was motoring back out of the door. And that couldn't happen.

Just then my human eyes became compound fly eyes. I didn't see Ax's tail snap through the air like a bullwhip.

I heard *fwapp*!

A soft impact sound followed, like someone had dropped oatmeal on the floor.

An extremely foul smell filled the room. I knew that smell.

<I think we are in trouble, Prince Jake,> Ax said.

<Is it dead?> Jake replied.

<In a manner of speaking,> Ax continued. <One half of it is consuming the other half.>

Taxxons are the universe's most dedicated cannibals. They don't just eat other Taxxons. They even eat *themselves*, given the chance. Hunger defines their world. In death, the Taxxon was acting out of some awful instinct.

<Ax,> Jake said, in his very calm, no-one-freak-yet voice. <Finish morphing to fly and let's

get out of here. Everybody stick close together. Hug the ceilings. Follow me. C'mon!>

We shot out of the room into a long hallway. The walls and ceiling of the corridor were black. The floor seemed to be an illuminated path. Four thin tubes of solid light hung where the ceiling met the wall.

<Ax, what are these lights along the ceiling?> Jake asked.

<Each colour designates the path to a certain portion of the ship. For example, on Andalite ships, following a green line will take you to the control room. A red line will take you to the engine room.>

<Do you think these light lines function in the same way?> I asked.

<It is likely. Everything the Yeerks have they stole from us. However, my fly vision cannot distinguish the colours of these various lines of light.>

<What would be the quietest part of the ship, Ax?> Cassie asked.

<Storage bays. They are most likely aft.>

<Can you tell which direction the ship is flying right now?> Jake asked.

<The ship is still heading north, Prince Jake.>

<So we want to go south. Let's do that.>

<Uh, a little warning before we make any turns, please?> I said. <In this light I can barely see a thing.>

<Ditto,> Tobias added.

<If we can't see each other,> Rachel said, <it's unlikely Visser Three and his walking woodchippers are going to see us. I think.>

<Think again,> Cassie said. <Look who's coming.>

A familiar blue blob. A now-familiar aroma.

<Stick to the ceiling,> Jake said.

Visser Three trotted right past us.

Right past us and into his room.

Then his voice was exploding in our heads like a nuclear bomb.

<Guards!> A moment's hesitation as he put it all together. Then, <The Andalite bandits! They are on board!>

The hallway was suddenly filled with the smell of Hork-Bajir.

<Ax, what light path do we follow?> Jake asked.

<I cannot be certain which leads to where. The Yeerk colour sense may—>

<JUST PICK ONE!> Jake roared.

<Follow me,> Ax said meekly.

Jake almost never yells. When he does, you have to know it's time to do what he says.

There were four lines of lights, and all of them looked the same hazy grey-green to me. To all of us. But Ax picked one.

<Get the Andalites!> the Visser screamed in an absolute frenzy of rage and excitement.

<Here! On my own Blade ship! Ah-hah! I will slowly kill the fool who fails me! Do you hear me? Get them! Get them! GET THEM!>

We blew out of there as fast as our little fairy wings would take us. We chased that ribbon of light, hoping it wasn't leading us into an even uglier death-trap.

Chapter 10

We found the storage bays. Ax led us there like he'd been born and raised on that Blade ship.

<They know about insect morphs,> Cassie said. <We're vulnerable. They could flood the ship with insecticide.>

<I'm not dying as a fly,> Rachel said. <They want me, I'm taking some of them down with me.>

She was already demorphing. And as far as I could see, she was right: forget dying as a bug. If the Yeerks were going to catch us, it wasn't going to be with a can of Raid.

We were about as trapped as we could get. Visser Three knew we were on his ship. It was only a matter of time. And as far as this battle was concerned, the Yeerks owned time.

In our normal bodies again we could see how scared we were. I could see the way Jake was gritting his teeth; Rachel's mean grin; Cassie's worry, tinged with sadness. It would almost have been better to remain in morph. In morph you could hear the fear, but you didn't have to look it in the eyes.

I was watching Rachel, trying to decide for the millionth time whether she was brave or just insane, when I happened to focus past her.

Rising up behind her was a pillar of glass. A cylinder three metres, four metres tall, and half as broad. Inside the cylinder was a vague shape, blood-red and midnight-blue slashes highlighting a glistening silver body.

Yes, body. Because despite the frosted glass and the mist that filled the cylinder, that three-metre-tall tube contained something biological. There was a row of the cylinders spaced across the cargo bay. Maybe ten in all.

"They look like creatures of some kind," Cassie said.

I could feel the cold emanating from the cylinders. I reached out to touch one, but my fingertips went numb before they'd got within two centimetres of the surface.

"OK, this is a totally unnecessary new weirdness," I said.

<They look almost like. . .> Ax began.

"Like what?" I demanded.

<I was going to say they look like the Venber Visser Three mentioned,> Ax said. <But they cannot be. . .>

"What's a Venber?" Rachel asked.

<An alien race from a frozen moon several dozen light-years from here,> Ax explained. <We learned about them in school. They were among the earliest evidence we obtained of life beyond our own planet. But the Venber have been extinct for thousands of years.>

"Yeah, well, speaking of extinct," I said, "we'd better get morphed or we're gonna end up the same way."

Cassie was trying to peer through the mist, struggling to get a closer look at the big, silver creatures. "What would Visser Three want with some extinct aliens? What do you know about these guys, Ax?"

<They never got beyond primitive tool use, though they may have had the intelligence to evolve further. Had they survived. They lived in very cold conditions — two hundred of your degrees below zero.>

"Now they're *our* degrees, too?" I muttered. "Hey, here's something to think about: the bad guys could be here any minute. Any one of *our* minutes. Do we want to spend the last few minutes of our lives talking about extinct alien ice-lollies?"

I must have sounded a bit hysterical. Jake actually smiled. "Marco's right. Get ready."

Suddenly Ax looked alert, like he was listening to far-off music. <We are descending. Possibly preparing for a landing.>

"Fine, whatever, let's morph," Jake said.

Descending? I wondered. *Preparing to land? Why would Visser Three let the ship land? If he landed, we could conceivably escape.*

A mistake?

I shook off the worry. I had enough worries already.

Minutes later, we were as ready as we were going to get. Jake was in tiger morph; Rachel was a grizzly bear; Cassie was a wolf; and Tobias and Ax were their own handsome selves. Me, I went gorilla.

Together we were a tough, deadly fighting team. And then. . .

Shwooof! To our left a door opened.

Shwooof! To our right a door opened.

Shwooof! A door opened right ahead of us.

Each door was big enough to frame a dozen Hork-Bajir. Peering over their shoulders were more Hork-Bajir.

And right then I realized why Visser Three had let the ship land: he'd located us. He knew he had us. And we were definitely dead.

Chapter 11

I stopped breathing. Hork-Bajir were everywhere. Everywhere!

This wouldn't be a fight. This would be a slaughter.

Then, at the centre door, *he* appeared.

<Well, well, well. Here aboard my own ship. How nice of you to come round to see me. Can I offer you anything? Something to drink? To eat? Or maybe just a quick death?>

The Visser laughed. He had reason to laugh. Three doors open and filled with Dracon-armed Hork-Bajir.

<Give the word, Jake,> Rachel whispered. <Give the word and I swear I can at least get *him.*>

Three doors? Wasn't there a fourth door? And why wasn't it open?

<Ax!> I said urgently. <I don't want to turn around and look, but is there a fourth door?>

Ax swivelled one stalk eye. <Yes! It must lead to the exterior of the ship. But there is a control pad protecting the emergency manual release. It is undoubtedly coded. It would take me hours to find the security code.>

Of course. And Visser Three knew that. But maybe this wasn't a case for subtlety. I flexed my canned-ham fist. <Jake! There's another door behind us. A keypad. Maybe I can break it open.>

<And get fried before you twitch,> Jake pointed out.

<No. The Yeerks will not fire weapons in here. Not with those canisters,> Ax said. <They are obviously valuable specimens.>

Jake reached a very fast decision. <Rachel. Next word Visser Three says, you slam the nearest canister. Marco? The keypad. Ax, back up Marco. Tobias, Cassie and me, straight at Visser Three, a feint.>

I was getting ready to make a lame pun about "feint" and "faint" when the Visser spoke.

<Surrender now and—>

Before he could get to his fourth word,

Rachel struck! A mountain of grizzly slammed hard into the nearest cylinder.

WHAM!

Nothing!

Too late, I'd already spun round and bounded towards the keypad.

<KILL THEM!> Visser Three screamed.

"Tseeeeer!" Tobias screamed.

"Hraawwwrrr!" Rachel bellowed. She slammed all her weight this time, all her strength.

Crack!

A single crack, a small, pathetic crack, appeared in the cylinder wall. The mist began to seep out.

Jake, Cassie, and Tobias attacked. No other option now.

I saw a flash of orange and black leaping straight at Visser Three. No less than half a dozen Hork-Bajir enveloped him, blades flashing.

I saw the keypad. I drew back my pile-driver arm and slammed it with all my might. It crumpled like a tin can.

<Rip away the metal!> Ax yelled, even as he used his reversed stalk eyes to aim a sonic-boom tail snap at a rushing Hork-Bajir.

Rachel withdrew, backed up about four metres, and ran all out, full speed, on all fours at the cylinder. A small army of Hork-Bajir leaped after her.

Just then, I saw Cassie flying through the air.

Not a leap. She'd been thrown, bloodied and broken.

Tobias was in the air, harassing Visser Three, aiming for his vulnerable stalk eyes.

WHAM!

Rachel hit the cylinder. A flailing mob of Hork-Bajir literally covered her.

And then the cylinder shattered.

CRASH! It fell in pieces.

Whoosh! The mist inside billowed out. Hork-Bajir screamed and tried to back away. But too late! The clouds of mist caught them, freezing any body part it touched.

Not freezing, as in it made them cold. Freezing, as in solid. Like stone gargoyles. I saw one puzzled Hork-Bajir gape in horror as his left leg simply broke off and lay on the deck like a piece of a statue.

The mist hit Rachel, too. But she had a thick coat of fur. The fur froze and shattered off like thousands of brittle needles.

I ripped away the loose metal of the keypad.

<Squeeze that handle!> Ax ordered.

I squeezed.

Too late, Visser Three saw his mistake. <Bridge!> he roared. <Bridge, get us up! Get us up!>

The outer hull door began to slide. It opened on to empty whiteness.

<Jake! Cassie! Everyone! Door open! Bail!> I yelled.

The freezing mist was swirling around the floor now, forcing the Visser to back up. But that didn't mean he wouldn't send his troops into it.

<After them! After them!>

Hork-Bajir ploughed through the mist and found themselves on frozen feet. Feet with toes that broke off, with ankles that snapped.

Jake coiled his tiger muscles and took the mist at a leap. Tobias was first out of the door. Cassie lay unconscious in a heap, with mist advancing on her.

Without hesitation, Rachel walked into the mist and lifted Cassie's wolf body with her teeth. The grizzly's left foot stayed where it had frozen. Rachel staggered to the door on a stump.

One by one, we tumbled out of the door and into emptiness.

Chapter 12

We landed about six metres below in a pile of fur, claws, wings and hooves. I hit hard, face-down. I was under hundreds of kilos of morphed humans and one alien.

There was a huge *whoosh.* The Blade ship, following Visser Three's orders and going for altitude. Bad timing. I could practically hear him screaming, <No, no! Down! Down!>

I scratched at the ground and tried to pull myself out of the squirming pile. But the ground was slippery.

Ice. I could feel the black, leathery skin on my chest burning against it.

Just a few centimetres from my face, I could see Jake's claws scraping at the ice.

I tried to push away, to get out from under

the grizzly bear lying over me. But not even my strength could move Rachel till she rolled away. I tried to stand up.

I felt my skin tearing as I pulled away from the ice.

<Ow ow ow ow!> I screamed.

But then I saw Rachel's foot. Or at least the stump where the foot had been. She was demorphing as fast as she could. Grizzlies can take a lot of pain. But nothing likes losing an entire foot.

Cassie was reviving, turning her wolf snout back and forth like a person having a bad dream. Then, <Yah! Oh! Oh, man! Wh-where are we?>

<Somewhere cold,> I said. <Really cold. You better demorph and remorph, fast!> I could see the Blade ship. It had shot into the air, up through the clouds, and was still hauling away. But it would be back.

<Marco's right,> Jake said. <Jeez! Is it cold enough?>

My arms were already starting to lose their mobility. It was intensely, horribly cold. The still-warm blood on my chest gave off a steamy mist in the frosty air.

I was a jungle creature. Big and furry, but not really adapted for anything less than hot and sticky. And we were a long way from hot and sticky.

Cassie was human again, standing barefoot

on ice. "Th-th-think I'll re-m-m-morph," she chattered. Rachel wasn't far behind her.

"What is this, Alaska?" she demanded, steam escaping from between her lips. As out of place as we all were, no one looked more out of place than Rachel in human form.

<Could be Alaska,> Tobias said. <About two kilometres that way I see some kind of base or even a town. Lots of grey, corrugated metal buildings. One bigger than the rest. Big doors like those on plane hangars. There's like this giant bowl attached to the roof. And that's the hawk report, boys and girls. I am morphing before I end up in the frozen foods section next to the frozen chicken.>

<That settles it,> I said. <It ain't Hawaii.>

I couldn't see the base in any detail. Just a vague outline in the distance. But to my right was an endless body of half-frozen water, a jigsaw puzzle in ice. On our left, a hundred metres from the shore, was a huge outcropping of craggy rocks, the foot of an enormous mountain range that swept up and away into the distance. No trees, no grass. Just a ridge of black rock and white snow.

<Not the Caribbean, either,> I said, trying to ignore the fact that my big gorilla feet were freezing in place.

<Oh!> Cassie cried. <I've never felt cold like this! I'm a wolf and I'm cold!>

<Tobias!> Rachel shouted. He had suddenly collapsed. He lay on the ice, flapping his wings lamely.

<I can't fly . . . can't morph . . . losing. . .>

Rachel scooped him up and tucked him into her chest with hands half-human and half-bear. She morphed, growing huge around him, all the while keeping him pressed to her fur.

I slapped my big hands against my arms and rubbed, trying to work feeling back into my fingers. I looked up and saw the Blade ship, an ominous black shape against the clouds.

<He is not coming back this way,> Ax said. <He will be heading for his base.>

You'd think that would make us feel better. But no one thought for a minute that he was just going to let us go.

No, he just figured there was no hurry. Unlike us, he knew where we were. And he knew we weren't going to get far.

Chapter 13

<We need to get moving,> Jake said. His tiger morph was doing fairly well, I suppose. Or else he was just refusing to complain. Which was fine. I'd complain for both of us.

<Ax?> Cassie asked. <How are you holding up?>

<I am holding nothing up,> he said. <But I am slowly freezing to death. I doubt I can maintain brain function for more than a few more minutes.>

<Ax, you really need to tell us these things,> Jake said. <Hang in for a few minutes. We need to move out. We need distance!>

I took off as fast as I could, which was pretty slow, considering I could no longer feel my feet. Every gust of wind felt like a punch in the face.

Tears streamed down my cheeks and froze before they reached my chin. The blood on my chest became a coating of pinkish ice.

We didn't get far.

Ax stumbled. <Prince Jake! I am not sure I can continue.>

<OK, look, um . . . OK, Ax! Tobias!> Jake commanded. <Neither of you has a good cold-weather morph. Morph to fleas and hide in Rachel's fur!>

<Come on guys,> Rachel shouted. <I've got you!>

Rachel stood over Ax while he began to morph. Tobias, still in her arm, began to shrink. Then Rachel scooped Ax's still-morphing form and held him to her chest as well.

<OK, now we move. We need distance, we need cover. Before the Yeerks can come out after us. Let's go!> Jake said.

We took off again, a staggering, miserable little gang of biological misfits. A tiger, a bear, a wolf and a gorilla.

I started giggling. Gorilla! Here in the snow. Funny.

Just tired. That was the thing. Tired.

I looked back up again for the Blade ship. Nothing in the sky. But the cloud above was kind of pretty. Looked like a horse. No, a unicorn. Yeah. Pretty.

We ran and kept running. Along the frozen

shoreline. Beneath the shadow of the gloomy rocks.

Every step was torture. My feet were numb, but the pain still burned in my legs. I ran on all fours, gorilla-style, and my knuckles were soon raw and bloody.

The wind came in sudden gusts, lashing my face, cutting straight through my fur. I hated the wind. It made me tired. Couldn't see right.

Just follow the orange kitty, I told myself. *Follow the big orange-and-black kitty.*

Take a thousand ice cubes, fill a bathtub with them, and crawl in. You might get a fraction of an idea what I was feeling.

Now imagine the prick of a very sharp pin. Imagine a solid sheet of pins slapped against your face. Again and again. That was the wind.

We ran on bloody frozen feet and now I saw rocks looming higher and higher beside me. Hide. Hide in the rocks. Yeah, that way the . . . the guys . . . the ones who were chasing us, wouldn't be. . .

I realized I was confused. The thoughts jumbling together in my head weren't making sense. Were they?

<OK, in here!> Jake said. <We can take a break.>

In where? Rocks all around us. Tall piles. Like . . . like rocks. Yeah.

<I cannot believe how cold it is,> Cassie panted, her breath turning to plumes of steam.

<I can barely feel my paws,> Rachel complained.

<What?> I said. <I need to sleep now.>

I looked down stupidly at my bare feet. Swollen. Huge. Nearly double their usual size.

I closed my eyes. Tired. Cold.

<OK, everybody,> Jake said. <We have to figure out what to do. Rachel, I know you're cold, but can you stand it?>

<For a while,> Rachel said. <Not for long. Aren't grizzlies usually hibernating in a cave somewhere in the winter?>

<Cassie? How about you?>

<Well, wolves are cold-weather animals, but I can't stand weather *this* cold. At least not for long.>

Not for long.

Voices. Faraway voices.

I dropped to the ground. And then I noticed I was on the ground. I had a sudden urge to stay there. Sitting on the frozen ground.

<Marco!> Jake yelled. <What are you doing?>

Everything was turning kind of grey.

<Marco, you have to keep moving,> Rachel shouted.

<What's happening?> Tobias asked from somewhere on Rachel's body.

<He's going into shock,> Cassie said, strangely calm.

<Marco!> Rachel yelled. She grabbed me with her big bear paws and shook me. <You've got to stand up!>

<Stop,> I mumbled. Angry. She's always angry.

<Marco, morph out!> Jake yelled at me. <Morph out!>

<Yeah.> I tried to nod.

Rachel shook me harder. <Come on, Marco! Don't lose it!>

But I wasn't listening. I didn't care. I was floating through space.

No, not floating. Flying. Just like an osprey. Through empty space.

Wait! A light up ahead. Calling to me. Drawing me to it. Very bright. Like . . . like the lights around the bathroom mirror.

I tried to flap my wings, but I didn't have any. I didn't need them. Not any more.

Chapter 14

<Marco!>

<I'm coming,> I whispered.

Almost there. Then everything would be perfect.

<Marco!>

<OK, OK . . . ooooo-kay.>

WHAM!

Something bashed me in the face. Blinding pain. I felt some teeth drop on to my tongue.

<Marco! Wake up!>

I opened my eyes. Jake, Cassie, and Rachel were standing over me. Rachel had blood on her big hairy paw. My blood. From my flat gorilla nose. Now somewhat flatter. Her paw was raised, ready to smack me again.

<Hey, hey, hey!> I yelled, gently touching my

crushed face with a frozen hand. <What is your problem?>

<I'm trying to save your life, you idiot,> Rachel said. <Don't know why, but I am.>

<Well, try a kinder, gentler method next time,> I whined, spitting out something that felt an awful lot like bloody teeth.

<We were losing you. You have to demorph, Marco,> Jake said. <Then remorph as a wolf. It's the best morph we've got for this climate. Rachel, you too, if you think it's best. I'll take Ax and Tobias while you go first.>

<They can stay on me,> she said.

<Um, Rachel?> Jake said. <You have to pass through human on the way to wolf.>

<Like we'd see anything?> Tobias said with a laugh. <We're fleas!>

I began to demorph. Slowly at first. Everything very slow. Brain not thinking too good.

I began to change, shrinking back to my normal size. My frozen, swollen fingers thinned. My black fur sucked itself back into my body, leaving me even more vulnerable to the cold.

A few seconds later I was back in my human form, with nothing on but a pair of black cycling shorts and a white T-shirt. Not a good body for the weather. I morphed swiftly to wolf.

Relief!

Not total relief. The wind still sliced through me with its cold steel edge. But I had fur that

was at least designed for fairly cold weather. And feet that were evolved for something other than padding around on heat-rotted vegetation.

Cassie demorphed and remorphed as a wolf. Rachel was right with her. Jake morphed as well. I know he'd suffered in his tiger morph. But Jake, being Jake, wouldn't complain till everyone else was safe.

<I think this is the best morph we have,> Cassie said thoughtfully. <Unless we get to open water. Then my whale morph would be good. I don't know about dolphin or shark. I think they're both more warm water. Still, these wolf bodies are not equipped for the Arctic or Antarctic or wherever we are. We might be able to survive for a few hours at a time, long enough to remorph and regenerate, but we're still vulnerable. Too vulnerable to be fighting.>

<Point taken,> Jake said. <We stay out of fights, if we can.>

I stuck my head out of the alcove to see what was going on back down the slope. With this slight elevation I could see the base clearly, if not in detail.

But it wasn't the far-off base that got my attention. There was very little alive anywhere near us, and thus almost nothing to smell. So when the new scent drifted our way, all our wolf heads perked up.

You probably know how well a dog can smell

and hear. Well, a wolf is to a dog what a Ferrari is to a Hyundai.

Smell! Sound! Sight! All locked on like some computerized targeting system.

<What the heck are those things?> I cried.

There were two of them. About two and a half metres tall. Humanoid. Torso, head, and limbs in the usual places. Only their heads were shaped kind of like a hammerhead shark's, oblong with big, dark globs on each side that must have been eyes. Each creature had two thick upper arms growing out of broad shoulders. The upper arms split at the elbows to make two forearms.

Big, burly, nasty-looking beasts. Silver, with flashes of blood-red and midnight-blue along their flanks, along their shoulders, and converging in their faces.

I'd seen that colour scheme before.

They were sliding towards us on long, ski-like feet. They used two of their forearms, one right and one left, to propel themselves forward.

And they glistened in the light like diamonds or crystals.

With their third and fourth forearms, each carried a chunky black tube of some kind.

<Ax, we've got aliens coming,> Jake said. <I think they're the ones we saw in those cylinders.>

Jake described them.

<I do not believe it,> Ax cried. <A perfect description of a Venber.>

<Venber? What happened to them being extinct?> I cried.

<Reports of their extinction may have been exaggerated.>

<Ax, are you developing a sense of humour? If so, stop it, OK?>

<Well, whatever they are, they're coming this way in a hurry,> Rachel said. <And judging by those big guns in their hands, I don't think they're welcoming us to the neighbourhood.>

<Yeah,> Jake said. <Let's get out of here.>

The Venber kept coming, making strange, crunching noises. Regular, repeated sounds that seemed to ricochet off the rocks behind us in a weird, distorted echo.

Crinch! Crinch!

Sproing! Sproing!

They seemed to know exactly where they were going. Or at least they knew exactly where we had gone.

<They're echolocating,> Cassie said. <Pinging us with those sounds.>

<Into the rocks,> Jake said. <They can't echolocate in there, can they?>

<They should not be able to now,> Ax pointed out. <We are already in the shadow of the rocks. This must be a very sophisticated sense to pick us out of the clutter. Very impressive.>

<Swell, you can ask one out on a date, Ax, you like them so much. Do you have anything *useful* to tell us?>

<Yes. They would have difficulty dealing with temperatures above freezing. Liquid water, for example.>

<Well, then we have nothing to worry about. We offer them a vacation in Florida and we're home free!>

<Marco, why didn't I just let you freeze?> Rachel wondered.

The Venber were about fifty metres away from us when they stopped. Then they raised those big tubes and pointed them our way.

They didn't look like cameras.

<I'm thinking we should duck,> I said.

Chapter 15

We crouched low, skulking wolves.

TSEEEEEEW! The horizon filled with a blinding green light.

About four tons of rock upslope from us became four tons of gravel.

Ka-BOOOOM!

It was gravel rain! Rock hail.

I've been shot at by Dracon beams before. They're pretty scary. These things were about ten stages past scary.

<Holy. . . !> Jake yelled. <What are those things?>

<Dracon assault cannons,> Ax replied. <They are used for attacking hardened ground facilities from orbit.>

<I am so out of here!> I cried.

<Forget the rocks, hug the shoreline,> Jake said. <They want a chase, we'll give them a chase.>

We took off along the dead rock and slush shoreline.

The Venber followed. Sliding along on their ski feet, pushing themselves forward with those massive forearms, they followed. Every few minutes one of them would stop and take a shot with its assault cannon, blasting the already lifeless scenery.

<Spread out,> Jake said. <One well-aimed shot could kill us all.>

We ran and ran down that shoreline. One good thing about being a wolf is the ability to run for hours without having to stop. A wolf can run all day and all night.

The Venber kept after us. They were bigger, they were stronger. We were faster. And they couldn't match our endurance.

But unlike the six of us, the two alien ice monsters didn't have to demorph every two hours.

<This makes no sense,> Ax said as we ran. <The Yeerks could not possibly infest the Venber. The Yeerks would freeze. They must be controlled by some other means. Unless, of course, the Yeerks managed to find a method of keeping themselves from freezing inside the Venber's body.>

<Whatever,> Rachel said. <Point is, we're out front. I don't even see them any more. Maybe they've given up.>

I turned to look over my shaggy grey shoulder. I couldn't see the Venber. Couldn't smell them, either, despite the wind blowing from behind us.

<No way they gave up,> Tobias said. <We have to keep moving.>

<So says the flea all nice and warm in his honey's fur,> I muttered.

<What did you say?> Rachel demanded. I suppose she was shocked that I'd dare to make any remark suggesting she and Tobias were more than just friends and Animorphs. Like that was some big secret.

We slowed our pace a little. My footpads were numb and swollen. Frostbite. Again. I couldn't feel the tips of my ears.

<We need to find somewhere to demorph and remorph,> Jake said. <What's our time?>

<We have twenty of your minutes left,> Ax replied.

I swear he emphasized "your" minutes. We trotted back over to the rocks that continued to follow the shoreline all the way to eternity.

We ran on till we found a deep, steep-walled alcove. It was still cold as the dark side of the moon. But at least the wind was left behind to howl and moan impotently.

We huddled around Cassie, trying to keep her warm as she demorphed first. Then we took turns demorphing and remorphing, huddling together like a litter of newborn puppies.

Weird. A bunch of wolves pressing flank to flank. It was a strange and kind of wonderful experience. It brought back memories I didn't know I had. From when I was very little. Sitting on the sofa with my mum, snuggled up against her, watching TV and sucking my thumb.

Corny. Probably the cold was getting to me. Or maybe it's just that in the cold, in an environment that is ready to kill you without thought or mercy, simple animal warmth, body and body, breath and breath, seems to touch something deep inside you. Millions of years of Homo sapiens, huddled together, body to body against the killing wind.

Until at last humans learned to make fire. Of course, that involved matches. Or at least sticks.

<So now what?> Rachel asked when we'd all remorphed. Ax and Tobias had remorphed as fleas and were hiding in Jake's fur. I suppose my undiplomatic remark about Tobias and Rachel had made them self-conscious.

<We have to keep moving,> Jake said. <I'm sure the Venber are still tracking us. But we also have to find somewhere to hide for the night. No way we'll survive this cold without shelter.>

<Maybe we can find a cave,> Cassie said. <Or a snowdrift and dig a hole in it for a lair.>

<Or a McDonald's,> I suggested. <I thought they were everywhere.>

<What we really need to do is find some cold-weather animals to morph,> Rachel added.

<I'll second that motion,> Tobias said.

When we were semi-thawed, our frostbite all replaced with healthy flesh in the new morphing, we moved on. It was getting dark. According to Ax it was only two o'clock — you know, in *our* hours. But the sun was already disappearing. That could only mean it was going to get colder.

Chapter 16

We trotted along the shoreline in the fading light. Sometimes we ran. Every once in a while I'd look back in the direction of the Yeerk station. I couldn't see anything. But now and then I caught a smell that I was pretty sure I recognized.

Venber. Still hunting us.

The ice along the shore was more solid here. It extended in a lumpy sheet from about three hundred metres to several kilometres from the shore. Beyond that, the water was thick with chunks of white.

Ax had said that water might be dangerous to the Venber, so we considered going right out on to the ice and closer to its outer edge. But if we stayed out in the open, the Venber

might be better able to track us with their echolocation.

And out on the ice there was no shelter at all from the terrible wind. We decided to stay closer to the slope of the ridge beside us. There, too, we'd be able to find cover in the rocks if it came down to combat.

The sun started to disappear on the horizon, giving the ice an orange glow. As the sun dropped, the wind shifted direction.

A sudden scent! Like a flashing neon sign to my wolf nostrils. Everyone caught the scent at the same time. We all stopped.

I sniffed again, concentrating, letting the wolf mind that existed beside my own provide a rough translation: a scent similar to Rachel's grizzly bear morph, but not quite the same.

I turned my ears towards the wind, towards the scent. Yes, just barely, I heard something. A steady, easy, confident gait. Ice and snow crunched by enormous weight. Four feet.

<Let me guess,> I said. <The Abominable Snowman.>

<Abominable something,> Rachel agreed. <Might be our dinner. Even a wolf needs to eat.>

We quickened our pace and began to turn in a wide arc towards the unseen creature. Cassie spotted him first as he emerged from the shadow of an ice heave.

<Over there,> she said.

My wolf's eyes locked on to a spot of black.

His nose.

Then two black dots above it.

His eyes.

The nose and eyes moved. And in the near darkness, the rest of him began to take shape. A humongous mass of off-white fur.

<Polar bear!> Cassie said delightedly. <I suppose that means we're Arctic and not Antarctic.>

<I did tell you our direction was north,> Ax sniffed from down deep in Jake's fur.

It was weird. This creature you only saw on TV or at the zoo: a polar bear. Sitting on the ice, scratching himself.

We stood there and stared at him. He stopped scratching and seemed to be staring back. He sniffed at the air, and then lifted his big bear butt and started lumbering towards us on four thick legs.

<I'm thinking that this guy is not going to be our dinner,> Rachel said.

<Two-to-one odds we end up being his,> I agreed. <Let's run away. Fast.>

<Uh-huh,> Jake said, starting into a trot.

<What is this polar bear?> Ax asked from Flea World.

<Polar bear,> Cassie said. <The largest land predator in the world.>

<What do you mean *largest* predator?> Rachel protested, as if Cassie had just insulted her. <I thought grizzly bears were the largest!>

<Grizzlies aren't true predators. Let's face it: you'll eat berries, given a chance,> Cassie answered. <Anyway, polar bears can actually be heavier, if they've really packed on the blubber. Although grizzlies are normally built thicker.>

<Just how much Discovery Channel do you watch, Cassie?> I asked. <No, I really don't want to know.>

<I could take him,> Rachel muttered. But she didn't sound too sure.

<Predators?> Jake said. <I thought bears just ate fish and berries.>

<Not polar bears,> Cassie replied, breaking into a full run now. <But this might actually be good news for us. Where there are predators, there are prey.>

The bear kept after us, lumbering along the ice in a casual way.

<What do polar bears eat?> Jake asked.

<Dumb kids playing hero,> I muttered.

<Seals, usually,> Cassie said. <Other things, too. But mostly seals.>

<I haven't seen any seals,> I said. We were running at full speed now. I looked back and saw the bear had slowed down. Apparently, we were not his main concern.

<Of course you don't see any,> Rachel said. <They're hiding from the polar bear!>

<Now that we're on this topic,> Jake said, <what exactly are *we* supposed to eat?>

<We could try fishing,> I suggested.

<I could use my grizzly morph,> Rachel said. <Grizzlies fish, right?>

<I doubt that'll work,> Cassie said. <Grizzly bears fish in streams. I don't think fish come anywhere near the surface in this part of the world.>

<Great,> I said, <so I suppose we just go ahead and starve. Why not? Everything else is going so well.>

Things were looking pretty hopeless: polar bear to the right of us, Venber behind us, and cold all around. And now it was almost completely dark. The temperature was beginning to drop from shockingly cold to hideously cold. And the wind was howling off the water.

<We'd better find somewhere to hide for the night,> Jake said.

<I'm just glad the Chee are covering for us back home,> Cassie said.

Usually Cassie knows the right thing to say. Not this time. The last thing I wanted to think about right then was my home, my warm home with my warm bed and my warm TV.

I've been hurled sixty million years into the past, and been trapped on alien planets, but I'd never felt so far from home.

Chapter 17

We dug a lair in a snowdrift on top of some rocks looking out over the ice. And by "lair" I mean a big hole. A big, wet snow hole.

<I get the bedroom with the separate bath,> I said. No one laughed.

For what felt like the tenth time that day, we demorphed, one by one. We shivered in our human bodies for just long enough to turn blue (all except Ax, who was already blue), then remorphed.

The temperature continued to fall. We heard the ice cracking and groaning like a never-ending thunderstorm echoing through the darkness. It was an amazing sound.

You know how they say all the continents used to be one big continent, and that over

millions of years they broke up and drifted apart? That's what it sounded like. The continents leaving each other behind.

We spent the night huddled together in our makeshift cave, trying to keep each other from freezing to death. Each of us took turns standing guard, which basically consisted of sticking a nose out in the frozen air every couple of minutes to catch wind of anyone or anything dangerous.

Once in a while, I caught a vague, alien scent.

The Venber were still tracking us. But as long as we were hidden underground, their echolocation would fail to find us.

<Say, Ax,> I said some time in the middle of the night. <You sleeping?>

<No, Marco,> he replied from somewhere on my chest. He and Tobias had moved after Jake began complaining of some suspicious itchiness.

<What's the deal with these Venber?> I asked.

<Every Andalite knows the story of the Venber,> Ax began. <In fact, the story of the Venber has much to do with the modern Andalite policies and methods of interstellar interaction.>

<Tell us the story, Ax,> Jake said. <Obviously, none of us can sleep. And we have

to demorph soon, anyway. So what do you know about the Venber?>

<Just what everyone knows,> he said. <I mean, what any Andalite knows. They were a primitive species with a highly unusual physiology. Unique, actually. They do not seem to have required radiant energy of any kind. Obviously they are not carbon-based.>

<Obviously,> I mocked.

<They were discovered back towards the dawn of Andalite space travel. Not by us, by some other race. The Five.>

<The five what?> Cassie asked.

<No one knows. They just called themselves The Five. No doubt it meant something to them.>

<Maybe they lived between The Four and The Six,> I suggested.

<Anyway, The Five discovered the Venber and began to trap and export them.>

<Say what?>

<They basically harvested the Venber. It seems that a Venber melts, burns, in any case becomes liquid at temperatures above freezing. And the resulting liquid has many uses. Particularly in the creation of superconductors for the primitive computers of that era.>

<But. . . But these are sentient creatures, aren't they?> Cassie asked.

<Yes,> Ax said simply. <They were. The Five

extinguished them. They annihilated a sentient species to speed their computers. The Venber disappeared.>

<That's sickening,> Cassie said. <That's just evil.>

<Yes,> Ax agreed. <But if it is any comfort, The Five are no longer in existence, either. Soon after we encountered them for the first time they . . . well, no one knows for certain what happened to The Five. But Andalites in that era were not the Andalites of today.>

There was a long silence after that. You couldn't say there was a chill in the air since it was already freezing. But our already low spirits had been ploughed under.

<Good bedtime story, Ax,> I joked. <If you ever have kids, they're going to need nightlights. Just one big question: if the Venber are extinct, why are they trying to kill us?>

<I can only speculate. I suspect that because of temperatures on Venbea, the Yeerks were able to retrieve some intact genetic material from Venber corpses.>

<So they regrew them?>

<Probably they coupled the Venber DNA with some other species. These would be a hybrid: part Venber, part something else.>

<What else?> Cassie asked.

Ax hesitated. <You would want to use a species with the most complex DNA structure

available. It would make it easier to attach new DNA.>

<And what creature would that be?> Tobias asked.

<Of the species available to the Yeerks?> Ax said. <Humans. Those Venber may be a hybrid of Venber . . . and humans.>

After that we fell silent and stayed that way.

We curled up against one another, four wolves and a pair of fleas, deep in a hole in the snow, lost in a frozen wilderness, thinking of far away tragedies on dark, frozen moons.

I'd have traded my left lung for a fire.

Chapter 18

Throughout the long, long night we demorphed and remorphed one at a time, time and again. We were *so* much more than exhausted.

Ax and Tobias started freaking out after a while. It was amazing they lasted as long as they did in flea morph. They demorphed and stayed for a while in their own forms, huddling between the four of us, regaining a sense of the reality they'd lost as nearly blind, bloodsucking fleas.

It was not a good night. It did not pass easily. I was cold, scared, hungry, cold, hungry and also cold. We were without a plan. Without a clue. As lost as it was possible to be. And more tired than I would have thought possible.

Morphing was probably the only reason we survived that night. After about an hour, the cold became so severe we thought we were going to die. The morphing process would bring us back to full health so we could start freezing to death all over again.

Many hours and many morphs later, the sun began to creep through the hole of our lair. I am not known as a morning person, but I was the first to crawl out and take a look. The temperature had risen. It was probably a balmy thirty below.

I sniffed the air and caught the scent of the Venber. <Those guys just do not give up!> I complained.

I smelled something else, too. Very close. Out on the ice a kilometre away.

The polar bear. It took me a while to find him. I couldn't see his black nose or eyes. When I finally did spot him, I realized why his eyes and nose weren't visible.

<Hey, guys, check this out,> I said. Jake, Rachel and Cassie crawled out of the hole and stood beside me at the look-out post. Jake was carrying Ax and Tobias again. They'd promised not to bite.

<I smell polar bear,> Cassie said. <But I can't see him.>

<Try a little to your right,> I said. Like this helped. The horizon was nothing but a vast sheet of white paper, with a dark edge where the water began.

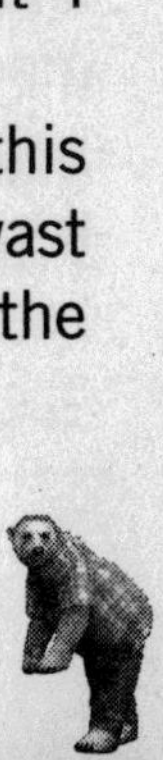

<Oh, I see him,> Rachel said. <What's he doing?>

Our pal had his entire head stuck in the ice, ostrich-style. He was a giant set of four pillar-like legs with no head.

<He must be seal hunting,> Cassie said.

We sat and watched him. The predator part of my brain was riveted.

We hadn't eaten anything for almost twenty-four hours. The extreme cold was sapping our energy badly. If we didn't get something to eat soon, we'd die. And the nearest fast-food place was probably two thousand kilometres away.

The polar bear pulled his head out of the water, shook it, and lumbered further out on the ice. Finally, when he was about twenty metres from the water's edge, he dropped on to his stomach and slithered along a metre or so at a time.

The polar bear stopped. He'd found something.

Suddenly he raised one of his giant paws and slammed it through the ice. I heard a desperate squealing and saw a pair of grey shapes scurry out of the hole his paw had made. The shapes scurried off and jumped back into the water a few metres away. The bear kept his paw in the hole, reaching around for the seal he'd trapped.

Then he stuck his head through the hole. He

stood up on his powerful legs. He raised his head. The seal was in his jaws. But the seal was too fat to fit through the hole.

He pulled it out anyway. The process made for instant, shredded seal.

<Oh my god!> Cassie cried.

<Geez,> Rachel said.

<I could have lived without seeing that,> I muttered.

<What happened?> Tobias asked. <What did he do?>

We watched him eat. He sat upright on his fat white back end, holding the big seal in both paws. He bit off huge chunks and gulped them down. Once he put down the seal carcass, scooped some snow off the ice, and used it to wash the blood off his face and paws.

It was disgusting. Even worse than some of the stuff you see in the school cafeteria. But I watched it greedily. I hoped he would leave us at least enough for a small meal.

<I think we have a situation here,> Jake said quietly. Calmly. His wolf tongue licked his wolf lips.

<Yeah,> Rachel said warily. <We have to eat, don't we?>

<We haven't eaten anything for at least a day,> I added.

I looked over at Cassie. She had to be freaked by what none of us had the nerve to

suggest we were suggesting. I mean, *I* was freaked by what we were not suggesting. But unlike Cassie, I wasn't willing to let my moral sense live while the rest of me died of starvation.

<Cassie?> Rachel said.

<What?> she replied, a hint of anger in her voice.

<What should we do?>

<Why are you asking me?>

I said, <We're not equipped to hunt in this environment, in these morphs. We're freezing. If we don't eat soon we'll be too weak to plan our next move, let alone finish what we came here to do. Destroy that satellite station.>

I know this sounds weird, but I'd kind of forgotten that we had a goal. All I'd been thinking about was staying warm and fed. And alive.

<But you're waiting for me to give my approval? Is that it?> she said.

<Look,> I began again. If I had to be the jerk in this situation, that was fine. I was used to it. I was usually the first one to state the obvious, no matter how ugly it was. Just call me Mr Ruthless. <In case you haven't noticed, there doesn't seem to be a McDonald's around here.>

<I noticed that,> Cassie said, a little annoyed. <It's obvious what we have to do. And

not just to the bear's leftovers, but to any *live* seal we can find. What I don't understand is why you're asking me for permission. Do you guys think I'd put an animal's life over yours? Or mine, come to think of it?>

<I don't know, I—> I started to say.

<You don't know? When did you start thinking I was some kind of fanatic? We're freezing, we're starving, and I'm going to go all tree-hugging, never-eat-anything-with-a-face on you?>

<Well, I can never tell what you'll think,> I whined, taken aback and feeling like I'd insulted Cassie.

<Here's a clue: don't kill a sentient creature except in absolute self-defence, try not to wipe out endangered species, and if you're going to raise animals for food, treat them as well as you possibly can. But when you're a wolf, a starving wolf wandering around the frozen Arctic, and you see a meal, eat it.>

Cassie is obviously not a morning person, either. This was grumpier than I'd ever seen her. Probably, despite her tough talk, she was not looking forward to eating cute seals for breakfast.

Come to think of it, I wasn't, either.

The two seals who'd escaped the bear were visible some distance off. We looked at them with the intensity of hungry wolves.

<Nature isn't pretty,> Tobias said, reassuring us. <It isn't supposed to be.>

<Yeah, survival of the fittest. . .> Rachel muttered.

<A good philosophy,> Ax said mordantly, <unless it turns out that the Venber are fitter than we are.>

Chapter 19

The bear eventually dropped the seal carcass, stood up on all fours, and lumbered away. When he was out of sight we walked to the blood-stained spot. Four wolves and two fleas.

The body was about a metre and a half long. The bear had left us plenty. In fact, it looked like he'd just ripped off the skin and chowed on the seal's blubber, leaving most of the meat for us. It was still steaming.

We stood there over it, looking briefly at each other and then back to the body. None of us wanted to take that first bite.

<Ax? Tobias? What about you guys?> Jake asked. They were both stuck on my skin somewhere.

<Actually,> Ax replied sheepishly, <I am not hungry.>

<Uh, me neither,> Tobias mumbled.

<What?> said Rachel. <How *can't* you be hungry?> Then: <Oh.>

<I apologize, Marco,> Ax said. <The flea's instinct was quite strong.>

<It's OK,> Cassie said. <It's no worse than what we're about to do.>

<Oh, yeah?> I said. <You can have them next, Cassie. You guys could've at least asked.>

<Let's just do this,> Jake said abruptly.

He stuck his snout into the carcass and tore off a stringy piece of the seal's flesh. We joined in after that, digging our sharp wolves' teeth into the already half-frozen body, tearing off chunks and gulping them.

<Say, Ax,> I said when I'd finished gorging. <Any idea where we are?>

<Far north,> he said.

<Northern Canada, Alaska, Greenland,> Rachel offered. <Iceland?>

<It may not be *the* Iceland, but it's an ice land,> Tobias said. <Past that, who cares?>

<We've got company,> Jake interrupted.

A couple of Arctic foxes were sitting on the ice a hundred metres away. They were about sixty centimetres long, with thick coats of long white fur.

<They'll just have to wait until we're done,> Rachel said greedily.

<Life's going pretty well, huh?> I said. <We're down to chewing seal bones. Not that I'm complaining. Any food is better than no food.>

<It could use salt,> Cassie said.

Coming from her, it was so unexpected we all burst out laughing.

<Salt? It could use a charcoal grill, some barbecue sauce and fries on the side,> Jake said. <And coffee. Hot coffee. I don't even drink coffee and I want some.>

Cassie stuck her nose in a drift and used the snow to wash the blood off her mouth. Then she rubbed her paws in the snow to wash them off, too.

<Now what?> Cassie asked.

<Yeah. Now what, Dad?> I asked Jake.

He sighed. <So far we're just getting chased. You don't win by running away. But first things first. We need to acquire some cold-weather morphs. We're barely surviving right now. We need the power to go on the offensive.>

<What do you think the odds are that our pal the polar bear will let us acquire him?> I asked.

Then my sensitive nose picked up the scent of seals, very close. Live seals. I spotted the two little grey balls floating in the water. They were the baby seals who'd escaped from the polar

bear. Looking right at us with those big black eyes.

They had faces like puppy dogs. Little heads with big eyes and whiskers. No ears. I usually like to reserve the word cute for myself exclusively, but there was really no other way to describe them.

<They're looking for their mother,> Cassie said.

Their mother? Their mother was. . .

A unexpected wave of emotion swept over me. Dumb, I know, but for two years I thought my mum was dead. Not the same, though. Was it?

Watching those little seals floating in the water, waiting for the mother who would never return, brought all the sadness back in a rush.

I moved between them and the horrible carcass on the ice. It wasn't our doing, killing their mother. But we'd profited from it.

<Our cold-weather morphs,> Rachel said. <Right there.>

Chapter 20

Jake came up with the plan. Cassie and I volunteered.

The job wasn't that hard, actually. While still on the ice, Cassie and I demorphed and remorphed into dolphins. We had to move fast. Dolphins are relatively warm-water animals, with no fur or blubber to help them deal with that kind of killing cold.

Then Jake and Rachel pushed us into the freezing water. I felt like one of those clowns you see on the news occasionally. You know — the ones who like to go swimming in the freezing winter ocean. In nothing but swimming trunks. The minute I hit the water I could feel my whole dolphin body, usually so full of energy and playfulness, go stiff and numb.

The seal pups barely even tried to escape. In any case, it was a vain try. Seals are amazingly agile, but we had the speed and the size and the intensity.

They dodged and weaved once or twice, but they were no match for us. I tried not to think about what that meant for their future. If they were no match for a couple of chilly dolphins, they'd be no match for the first killer whale or polar bear to come along.

Cassie and I grabbed one in a perfectly executed, acrobatic manoeuvre. We came up swiftly behind him and each grabbed a flipper.

The pup struggled, but this was a case of Great Dane versus Chihuahua. He did, however, manage to scratch me on the nose a few times with his tiny teeth. It drew blood. It hurt, and it felt good. I felt like I deserved it.

After we'd got a good grip on him with our mouths, being careful not to hurt him, we pulled him back to the others. They'd started to demorph when they saw us coming back.

We nosed the little seal up on to the ice. Up at the feet of a strange little collection of unlikely creatures: two humans dressed for an August day, a red-tailed hawk shifting from talon to frozen talon on the ice, and Ax.

Jake and Rachel grabbed the pup and held him between them. First one, then the other, acquired the pup's DNA. They held him still as

Ax pressed his many-fingered hand into the wet fur. Tobias fluttered up and landed on Rachel's shoulder. A painful thing for Rachel, though by then she was too cold to feel the bite of the talons.

The seal pup looked up, mystified but amused at the winged creature who gingerly touched him with his talon.

Cassie and I propelled ourselves up out of the water and demorphed on the ice. Not a pleasant experience. My skin froze to the ice halfway between dolphin and human. I ended up leaving a centimetre or so of Marco behind.

"Have I mentioned that it's cold?" I shivered, human once more. I touched the seal. Wet and firm and soft. Like touching a furry water balloon.

"Sorry," I said, for no good reason.

"Nothing we can do," Cassie said. She set the pup back down on the ice. He scooted to the water's edge and slid in, rejoining his — or her — brother or sister.

"They might m-m-make it," Rachel chattered.

But Cassie shook her head. For some reason she smiled sadly at Tobias. "No, they won't make it. But they'll feed some orca or polar bear, and you can't go all mushy over these guys without realizing that orca babies and polar bear babies have an equal right to live."

<Still, if we could. . .> Tobias said.

They were remembering the skunk litter we'd once saved. Tobias had eaten one of the skunk kits. Then he'd helped Cassie keep the rest alive.

"Nature, huh?" Rachel said.

<Yeah. Nature,> he replied. <Suppose we better morph.>

"Or we could just stand here and freeze solid while discussing survival of the fittest," I said. I was hopping from bare foot to bare foot, trying not to let either freeze to the ice.

Rachel gave me one of her patented, insolent smiles. "You in a hurry, Marco? Has it oc-c-c-ccurred to you yet that if those little guys are some killer whale's meat, we w-w-will be, too?"

That had not occurred to me. Now it was occurring to me in vivid colour with sound effects. "That's a happy thought, Rachel."

"Always here for you, Marco," she said. But already Rachel was changing.

I focused my cold-addled brain on the new image of the seal. And then, slowly at first, I began to morph.

My arms began to shrink. Smaller, smaller. Weird doll-sized replicas of arms that shrank till they were no more than eight centimetres long.

My fingers shrunk, too, but from the tips grew long, ice-gripping claws. The fingers melted together, then instantly separated again, drawing a thin web of flesh between.

My legs were almost disappearing. I knew I was going to fall, but it still surprised me when I suddenly just plopped over, face-first, on to ice. My feet shrank and narrowed and transformed themselves into the seal's flippers.

All the while my torso was growing smaller and yet chubbier. Blubber bubbled up beneath my skin. It was a little like that movie with Eddie Murphy, *The Nutty Professor*. Like that, only on a smaller scale.

I heard squishy sounds as my internal organs twisted around to fit my new body. My bones cracked and groaned, reshaping themselves to form my new skeleton. I was now an over-inflated football with flippers.

On my still-human face I grew long whiskers. My ears shrivelled up and into my skull, leaving just a pair of holes. My head was no bigger than a baseball, while my nose stretched itself out until it was shaped like a puppy's.

I looked out at the frozen world through large, dark eyes and discovered that they saw about as well as my human ones.

Finally, short, thick fur sprouted all over my body, rippling across my chest and down my back like I was a soft toy.

And then . . . and then. . .

Oh! The joy! The blessing! The fabulous, incredible, sensuous sensation! The most wonderful thing I have ever felt from the day of my birth to that very moment.

Warmth!

I was warm! Warm! If the heavens had opened and a giant hand had come down out of the clouds, giving me a billion dollars, my pick from the entire cast of *Baywatch* — past and present — and allowing me to grow sixty centimetres taller while magically acquiring all of Michael Jordan's skill with a basketball, I could not have been happier.

I! Was! WARM!

Cold? What cold? There was no cold.

I was on the beach at Malibu, sipping lemonade and gossiping with Tom Cruise.

I felt other things, of course. The seal's instincts were all there: an urge to run, an urge to chase fish, yadda yadda, but come on, I was warm!

My whiskers were amazingly sensitive. They felt even the slightest change in wind, the slightest movement from anyone else in our group. And part of me was still sniffing for my mother, but I, Marco, was the one in control. And I, Marco, was warm.

Did I mention I was warm? And happy? For about three seconds.

<The Venber!> Tobias yelled, blowing my happy mood away.

<Where?> Jake snapped.

TSEEEEEEEEW!

A huge bolt of blistering light hit the ice not a metre away. If it had hit rock, we'd have been blown apart in the shrapnel explosion.

But it hit a patch of perfectly smooth ice.

SHWAAANGGG!

Ricochet! The Dracon cannon blast hit at a low angle, hit reflective ice, bounced, and blew a hole in the side of the ridge behind us.

It was a one-in-a-million shot. We decided not to try for two.

<Run! Dive! NOW!> Jake yelled.

Run. Yeah, right, no problem. I spun my ball-shaped body. We were only a few metres from the water, but it seemed like a kilometre with these weird little legs. No, not legs. Feet. Feet with no legs. Not a good land-going combination. I shuffled my fat belly right and left, right and left, and inched towards the water.

It probably looked funny. It didn't feel funny.

TSEEEEEEW!

Ka-BOOOM!

A miss, but not by much. Water and ice rose in a column behind us, a geyser at subzero temperatures.

<They must have just seen us morph!> Cassie said.

<Maybe they just really hate seals,> I said. But even in my panic I realized the importance of what Cassie had said. If the Venber knew we

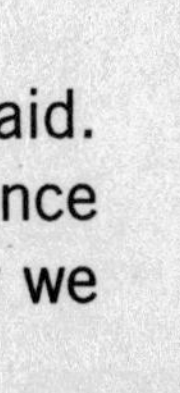

were human, we couldn't allow them to reach the Yeerks again.

I shuffled my fat belly over the ice, picked up momentum, saw the water's edge, kicked frantically and. . .

The next cannon blast blew the spot where we'd been into ice cubes.

But by then, I was in the water.

Chapter 21

As awkward as our seal bodies were on land, they were perfect for the water. We couldn't swim as fast as dolphins, and our tail flippers weren't as efficient as a dolphin's tail, but we cruised, using our front flippers as rudders.

<We should be safe under the surface,> Jake said. <There's no way they can follow us, right, Ax?>

<I believe not, Prince Jake,> Ax replied.

I noticed one of the others doing it first. Making little clicking noises. Echolocation. Like dolphins. Like bats. Like Venber.

I shot off a few clicks of my own. What bounced back was an amazing picture of my surroundings: every fish, every plant, several

other seals close by, every chunk of ice floating on the surface.

We swam for maybe half an hour. Back towards the Yeerk base. Back towards our mission, long-forgotten in the rush to stay alive.

It was also, we hoped, a good tactic. We would be doubling back on the Venber. With any luck at all, they'd search the ice for us till they became extinct. Again.

<Did they see us? I mean, as humans?> I asked.

<Why else would they take a shot at a bunch of seals?> Tobias wondered.

<Great. Now we have a whole new problem,> Rachel said. <We can't let them reach the Yeerk base.>

<Go kick their butts, Rachel. Let me know when you're done.>

<There is a way to ensure that these Venber do not connect with the Yeerks,> Ax pointed out. <Destroy the Yeerk base.>

<Yeah, 'cause that'll be so easy,> I said.

<Wipe out the base, we eliminate the problem,> Jake reasoned. <Kill two birds with one stone, as they say. Sorry, Tobias,> he added as an afterthought.

We stopped twice to surface and catch a breath. Seals can only hold their breath for about ten or fifteen minutes. We spy-hopped up through holes in the ice, but the frozen monsters were nowhere to be seen. Neither were any bears.

For the first time since we'd landed in this godforsaken place, I felt almost comfortable. I should have known the feeling wouldn't last.

<Here they come!> Cassie yelled.

For a split second I didn't know what "they" were, but then I felt a vibration in my whiskers and knew the threat came from the water.

That meant one thing.

Orca! Killer whales!

<MOVE! MOVE! MOVE!> Jake screamed.

We moved. But then, down through the murk of water, I saw them. Twin submarines in white and black.

Willy: free and looking for a seal meal.

<Oh, man,> Tobias groaned. <They're on us!>

<These are very large creatures,> Ax said with more than a little panic in his voice.

<Yeah, they are,> Rachel replied. <And I think they've got big appetites, too.>

I pumped my rear flippers as fast as I could. Above us, sheet ice. A hole! We needed a hole!

There! Light!

I shot towards the hole. I saw the others converging with me.

One, two, threefourfivesix, we blew through the hole, into the air and landed on ice.

Mad scrambling to get away from the hole, crazed, clumsy scrabbling. But then I looked down. Down through the ice I saw a black-and-white smile.

I could see the orca. Which meant. . .

<Cut left!> I yelled.

Crrrrrack! Pah-LOOOSH! The huge, blunt snout exploded through the ice like a scene out of *Hunt for Red October*.

Right beside me! The ice rose up, a brand new mountain. I slid down the steepening slope and motored my pathetic claws.

Crrrrrack!

The second killer whale erupted, not three metres in front of us. They were working together. Trapping us.

<I am so totally sick of this mission!> I shouted.

<Morph!> Cassie yelled. <They hunt seals, not humans.>

Great advice. But try demorphing when the Navy from Hell is popping up all around you, grinning big toothy grins and eyeballing you like you're a cheeseburger.

I scrambled and slid and began to emerge into my human shape.

The orca behind me dropped down into the water, then shot — if you can picture a black-and-white sausage the size of a stretch limo shooting — straight up.

Over my head and dropping towards me!

Any normal seal would have kept going in a straight line, and any normal seal would have been lunch. But I had a human brain. I dug one claw into the ice and spun to my right.

A huge load of sleek blubber landed with a crash centimetres behind me. Mouth open, the orca was ready to snap me up.

Only I wasn't there any more. And by the time Willy spotted me again, I had very cold arms and very cold legs and was hobbling away like some hideous freak of nature.

Willy thought that over. He decided he didn't want to be eating anything that looked quite like me.

The two seal-killers slid back down through the ice and went off about their murderous day while I stood there, demorphing and shaking and shivering and chattering out words I can't repeat here.

I saw the others, spread out over a hundred metres or so, all in their normal bodies, all looking about like I felt.

"Is this just the absolute armpit of the universe?" I demanded.

"Ask him," Rachel said.

Only then did I notice that everyone was not staring at me. But past me.

I turned. And I said, "Hi. Um . . . no offence about the armpit thing and all."

"None taken," he said.

Chapter 22

I suppose I expected him to run. But he didn't. He just stared at me, then at the others, then back at me.

He was sitting in a beat-up little fishing boat with a small outboard motor. It suddenly occurred to me that he'd probably scared the killer whales off with his engine.

I kept looking at him. He kept looking at me. I didn't know what to do. Or what to say.

So I waved and said, "Hi. How's it going?"

He didn't say anything for a minute. Just stared. Finally he said, "You some kind of spirit or something?"

I put my frozen hand on my frozen chest. "A spirit? What makes you say that?" I made a lame attempt at laughter.

He grabbed his oar and paddled closer.

He had a large, round face, with slightly slanted black eyes and skin like well-worn boot leather. Inuit, I guessed, what with this being the frozen north. In any case, I was pretty sure he wasn't French.

He was wearing a weird combination of clothes. Trousers made of fur, mittens made of some other kind of fur, and a shabby, big, blue anorak.

"You look cold," he said when his boat had touched the edge of the ice. "I didn't think animal spirits got cold. You want a blanket?" He held up a huge piece of fur, dark grey and silver with light grey rings. The same kind of fur I'd been *in* just two minutes ago. I took it and wrapped it round myself and under my feet while he drove a spike into the ice's edge, anchoring his boat.

"How about your friends?" he asked. "They animal spirits, too?"

"I suppose so."

He eyed me with more curiosity than fear. More interest than scepticism. He wasn't much older than I was. It seemed weird that a kid so young would be out all by himself in the middle of nowhere.

Of course, I wasn't one to be calling anyone else weird.

"My grandfather used to talk about animal

spirits all the time. I just thought he was crazy." He spun his finger around his ear in that universal gesture of insanity. "But I always told him, 'Yeah, that's right, Grandpa.'"

"Uh-huh," I said, covering my ears from the freezing wind. "I mean, you never can tell, can you?"

He stared some more. "Tell your friends I have more pelts."

"He has pelts!" I yelled a little too loudly. "How about if you guys all come on over and have some nice, warm pelts?"

Not that I was worried. Not that I needed company.

The others came closer.

The guy began handing up sealskins out of his boat. They were piled high. But a number of them looked as if they'd been burned. Scorch marks parted the fur.

"Are you an eagle?" he asked Tobias, peering curiously at him.

<A hawk, actually. A red-tail. We're a very common species.>

"Not round here. The birds round here don't talk." Then he focused intensely on Ax. "What are you?"

I could almost hear everyone sigh in relief. If this guy was a Controller, he would (a) know an Andalite when he saw one and (b) stay far, far away.

<I'm an Andalite.>

"You a common species, too?"

A joke! I decided to like the guy. Besides, anyone who could be this laid-back about running into our little freak show had to be all right.

"That's a lot of sealskins," Cassie said, huddling within one herself.

"Yeah. A lot. Not so good, though. All those burned ones, barely worth hauling to the trading post. And anyway, they'll come off my quota. Bad."

"How did they get burned?" Cassie asked, already knowing the answer as well as I did.

"Those crazy *Star Trek* men. Shooting seals with phasers and all. Like those people are using them for target practice or something. They show no respect. Makes me mad."

"*Star Trek* guys?" I said.

"Yeah," he replied. Then, "Oh, I suppose you animal spirits don't watch TV, huh? You need to get a satellite dish, Spirit-boy."

"The name's Marco. That's Jake, Rachel, Cassie, Tobias . . . he's the one with the wings . . . and Ax. Ax isn't from round here."

"Hi. I'm Derek."

"Derek?" I don't know what I expected to hear, but it wasn't Derek.

"Are you all alone out here?" Cassie asked.

"Yeah."

<How far away is your home?> Tobias asked.

"Oh, a ways." He cocked his head towards the west. The kid was talking to a bird. But he didn't even flinch. "Coupla days."

"A couple of days?" Jake said.

"Sure. I go on hunts every year," he said. "Since I was a kid."

"And you hunt seals?" Cassie asked, her voice level.

"Yeah." Derek cocked his head. "You don't like hunting?"

"Well . . . not like the crazy *Star Trek* guys."

"Hunting for sport. Like it's a game. Yeah, we get guys come up here for that. Up from New York and Detroit. Shoot bears and caribou from helicopters. No respect for nothing, those guys. Those guys at the station, though, they're the worst. They're just crazy for killing." He cocked his head. "That must make you animal spirits mad."

"We . . . we never exactly said we were spirits," Jake said.

"No? So what are you, then?" he asked. "Aliens?"

"He's an alien," I said, pointing at Ax. "The rest of us are just idiots."

The guy smiled. His expression hardened. He didn't like not getting answers. "You have something to do with that station they're building? With those big ice creatures? With the spaceships?"

I shot a look at Jake. He shrugged.

"Yeah, we have something to do with them," I said.

"Yeah?" he answered. "Well, I don't like them. What are they doing up there, anyway? They aren't any of those ecology people come up here sometimes. They aren't hunters, either. They're making a mess in the water. Scaring away everything with their noise and their weird guns. Who are they? Who are *you*?"

"I suppose you could say they're the bad guys," Jake said. "And we're the good guys. We came here to destroy that station."

"Sounds good to me," Derek replied. Like it was no big deal. Like we'd just suggested a visit to the local 7-Eleven. "I hope you do. I worry Nanook's gonna stick his big nose round there and end up getting it shot off or something."

"Nanook?" Jake said. "Who's Nanook?"

"Nanook's my friend. You don't know Nanook?"

"Uh, should we?" I said.

"You must've seen him," he continued. "He's been around here the last few days. I've been following him. I like to watch him work. He's a very great hunter."

"Maybe we have seen him," Jake said, puzzled. "What does he look like?"

"Well, he's pretty big, with white fur," he began.

"Oh, *him*!" Great. The Inuit comic. "Yeah, we've seen him."

"You've been hunting *him*?" Rachel said. "With *that*?" She pointed at the rifle in the bottom of his boat. And his short spear. "You're going to need more firepower."

"Not hunting him. Tracking him. Nanook's my buddy. Known him since I was a kid."

"Well, here's a really insane question," I said brightly. "Do you think we could stroke him?"

Chapter 23

We didn't have to go far to find Derek's friend Nanook.

We morphed back to seals, followed Derek's boat, and found the polar bear sprawled on the ice on his back, lounging in the sun. Like he was at the beach. Frankly, it annoyed me. How could any creature enjoy this place?

We crawled up on to the ice a few hundred metres away from the bear and demorphed to human.

"I wish I could do that," Derek said, watching with interest as human faces appeared on seal bodies.

We'd been careful to stay downwind of the bear. We'd been chased enough.

The plan was simple. The kind of plan we

come up with when we just can't think of anything smart or subtle.

"So you're going to just go and grab old Nanook?" Derek asked sceptically.

"Yeah. Why? Something strange about that? Something totally, absolutely INSANE about that?" I asked.

<That is sarcasm,> Ax helpfully explained to the Inuit.

"Yeah," Derek said. "I thought maybe it was."

I looked at Rachel. She and I had the fun part of this plan.

She grinned her Xena grin. "OK, Marco, yes, even I think this is insane."

She was already morphing. Growing huge-shouldered, with rail-spike claws and shaggy brown fur. I was morphing, too. Back to gorilla. The only other morph we had that could help with this particular plan.

Together our little gaggle advanced on the polar bear. A grizzly, a gorilla, a bird, an alien and two humans wrapped in seal pelts.

Derek stayed behind. He didn't offer any explanation. None needed: he was sane. When you're the only sane one at the lunatic picnic, you don't have to explain.

The polar bear abruptly rolled over. "He's noticed you," Derek called out from his safe distance.

Jake, Cassie, Ax and Tobias all hung back. Rachel and I kept going forward.

<This whole thing would be killer on Pay-Per-View,> I said. <Extreme Fighting: two bears and King Kong.>

<I go straight at him. You grab him from behind.>

<Yep.>

<Ready?>

<Nope.>

<GO!> Rachel yelled, and we were off at a slipping, sliding, panicked, pants-wetting-if-I'd-had-pants run.

Bear-to-bear! The polar bear didn't even flinch. Rachel dropped to all fours and slammed into the other bear's shoulder. Brown on white.

Whumpf!

"Hrrroooowwwwr!"

"Hrrroooowwwwr!"

Raking claws! Snapping jaws. The two bears were up on their hind legs now, swinging away like a pair of super heavyweights.

Rachel was not winning. She wasn't losing, but she was also not winning.

She shoved. The polar bear shoved back. Rachel landed on her back.

It was a shocking sight. I hadn't thought there was anything strong enough to knock a grizzly down. I saw a spray of blood across the polar bear's white chest. Rachel's blood.

I was in a loping run, trying to get round behind the big white monster, but the two bears were up again, on all fours, circling, circling, lunging!

WHAM!

<I could use some help here!> Rachel yelled.

The polar bear was a hair taller, maybe heavier, too. On the other hand, he was just a bear. While Rachel was human. Well, at least her brain was human.

The polar bear rose to its full height, ready to come crashing down on Rachel. That's when Rachel rolled into it. Not a bear move.

The polar bear went down, tripping over Rachel to slam jaw-first into the ice.

<Hah!> Rachel yelled. <Now I don't want your help, Marco. I'm taking this guy down myself.>

I considered it for a split second. But I was pretty sure Jake would not approve. I leaped forward and grabbed the polar bear's right arm.

He shoved himself off Rachel and swung his arm to throw me off. He didn't throw me off. But he did fling me into a nearly flawless double axel.

I kept my grip, but let me tell you something:

polar bears are strong. Gorillas are so strong they can rip saplings out of the ground. And this guy was stronger.

I held one arm and Rachel slammed directly into his belly, headfirst.

The polar bear went "wooof!" and froze for just a second while he sucked wind. The second was enough. I grabbed his other arm — well, leg actually — and pinned him in a sort of full nelson.

Rachel wrapped her own big paws around him and together we wrestled Hulk Frozen to the ice.

Tobias swooped down out of the sky, complaining about there being no lift at all in this cold air. Like that was the major drama.

He sank talons into Derek's friend Nanook and began to acquire him, while Rachel and I lay panting and counting our wounds. The bear went into the acquiring trance and a few minutes later we all had his DNA floating around inside us.

We let the bear go and ran like ninnies back to the water's edge.

"That was cool," Derek said. "This will make a great story for me to tell. No one will believe it, but it will be a great story."

Nanook the polar bear went lumbering off. No doubt to tell some stories of his own. I could hear it now: "No, seriously! A gorilla. I'm minding my own business, and suddenly there's this gorilla. . ."

Chapter 24

We left Derek. He said there was a storm on the way. So we said good-bye and let him go to tell whatever stories he wanted to tell. If he told a Controller he'd seen humans morphing, it would be trouble. But it occurred to us that an Inuit village in the middle of absolute nowhere was probably not high on the Yeerks' list of places to take over.

We had morphed the polar bear, giving Derek one last bizarre performance. *Star Trek*? Hah! He wouldn't be seeing this kind of thing on his satellite dish any time soon.

Now we were feeling pretty good. Better than we had since arriving here in Freeze Pop World.

We had *the* morph for this place. Like being

a tiger in the jungle or a crocodile in a swamp, we owned this place now.

Owned it!

I've been a gorilla. I've been a rhinoceros. I've felt power before. But this was new.

I stood nearly three metres tall, reared up. I weighed maybe a thousand kilos. And if those numbers don't mean anything to you, think about it this way. I was a metre taller than Shaquille O'Neal. I weighed *five* times as much as him.

I could have dribbled Shaq the length of the court and stuffed him. I was mighty. I was seriously mighty.

My front paws were thirty centimetres wide. Each had five webbed toes with long, black claws. My powerful front legs could have flipped over a pick-up truck.

And the cold?

What cold? If the thick layer of blubber underneath my skin wasn't enough, my body had made other adaptations for warmth.

My fur looked white, but it wasn't. It was transparent. Transparent and hollow. Every bristle was like a little greenhouse, turning sunlight into warmth, which was absorbed by my black skin.

I could see just as well as I did as a human, maybe a little better. Far better than poor Rachel in her grizzly morph. My hearing was

only average, but my sense of smell was awesome. I could smell seals all over the place.

Not much else *to* smell, when you think about it.

The bear mind that lay just beneath my human consciousness was no bubbling stew of emotions, no panic, no fanatic hunger. Nanook was calm. Completely without fear. What was there to fear?

He could go for weeks without eating. Hunting was more about play than survival. He actually spent more time lounging around than he did looking for food.

We sauntered back towards the Yeerk base with the cockiness of Clint Eastwood going into the town saloon.

It was a long walk, punctuated by refreshing plunges into the icy water. We ended up having to demorph, of course, and that was no fun at all. But then it was back to being Lords of the Ice.

<Looks like Derek was right about the storm,> Tobias said.

The wind was pretty bad by the time we came in sight of the Yeerk base. No new snow was falling, but the drifts were being whipped up and thrown around. Visibility was dropping fast.

<It may be helpful to us,> Ax suggested.

Jake was surveying the kilometre of scenery

ahead between us and the base. <I'm thinking we approach from the water. Last direction they'd expect an attack to come from.>

The base came to within a hundred metres or so of the water at one point. It was a collection of corrugated steel buildings, an unattractive bunch of structures placed seemingly at random. There were vehicles — Sno-Cats and big trucks and motorized cranes. Nothing alien to the casual observer. Unless you happened to notice the big silver Venber, bending steel with their bare hands as they built the main satellite dish.

<What do we do about them?> Cassie wondered.

<Try and stay out of their way,> Tobias suggested.

<How about afterwards?>

<Take them home and make them pets?> I suggested.

<They *are* a unique species,> Ax said. <They may not be pure Venber, but I would dislike being the latest to exploit and destroy them.>

I said, <You know, fearless leader, it occurs to me we're big tough bears and all, but just exactly how are we supposed to destroy that base? Maybe we'd better focus on that first.>

Chapter 25

Night was falling. Gloom spread slowly over the lake, turning the ice a ghostly blue. At the base, the lights came on. The Venber didn't need them, but the human-Controllers in their Michelin Man anoraks did.

We came with the night. Moving as silently as we could, single file so that at a casual glance a person might only see one bear.

We had a plan. The four fateful words that usually end up meaning a lot of yelling, screaming, mayhem and madness.

One thing we knew. Or hoped we knew: Visser Three was not at the base. Not even the big hangar building could have contained his Blade ship. That was some relief. Unfortunately, the Venber were there. They worked on, oblivious to changing light. Heedless of the plummeting temperature.

They knew we were out there on the ice. Knew at least that a bear was out there. We kept our line straight. Would their echolocation show more than one shape? Would they have the wit to sound an alarm?

There was no way to know, as we crunched across the ice, staring at one another's big bear butts. Jake in the lead. Tobias behind him. Then me, Cassie, Ax and Rachel.

Closer and closer, in slow motion. No running. No sudden charge. Just that slow, steady, lumbering walk.

We were totally exposed. No cover. Nothing at all between us and a well-aimed Dracon blast. The Venber we saw weren't armed. They were wielding tools, carrying, shaping, twisting. But the Dracon cannon couldn't be too far off.

It was like one of those Civil War battles. Walk, walk, walk, standing upright, no dodging and weaving, just walking steadily towards death. Nothing you could do about the bullet that blows a hole in your heart. Nothing.

Closer and closer. We could hear their heavy footsteps. We could smell their strange, chemical smell. I could see the effortless power as they worked.

One of them swung his big hammerhead

around and seemed to look right at us. But that was it. Just a look.

And now we were practically among them. Venber to the left. Venber to the right. I had stopped breathing. Our little single-file subterfuge was all over. They could see plainly that we were six great big bears.

No reaction. Work continued. We kept walking while my brain screamed the word "ambush!" over and over.

Suddenly a door opened. A rectangle of light. Loud human laughter. A man or woman — who could tell? — in a huge anorak stepped out onto the ice. And froze.

She stared at us. We kept moving. No one here but us bears, ma'am. Nothing to worry about. Just a little bear parade.

"ALARM!" she screamed. Definitely a she. "ALARM! ALARM!"

<The hangar!> Jake ordered. <Go for the hangar!>

We broke into a run. And we could put on speed when we needed to.

Past the Venber!

The big hangar door was shut and locked, but we barrelled towards it, heedless of the searchlights that snapped on everywhere. Heedless of the human-Controllers pouring from the buildings.

"Andalites in morph!" someone yelled. He

sounded in control. Not panicked. He sounded like a guy with a big stick to swing. "Program the Venber! Target: any quadruped. Over-ride all security protocols. The Andalites must not escape."

Program the Venber?

<That explains much,> Ax said.

It explained diddly to me, but maybe I was just too busy thinking about what a creature who could twist steel like it was spaghetti could do to me.

<Keep moving! Side door! Side door to the left!> Jake commanded.

To my left, a slight figure. Another woman? A kid? She stepped out, carrying what I would have sworn was a TV remote control. She was calmly punching keys on the thing.

<Here they come!> Rachel yelled from the back of our disordered line.

We knew who "they" were.

The Venber dropped their tools, dropped their sheet metal and steel rods, and broke into a loping, swoosh, swoosh, swoosh, cross-country skiing run. Five of them! No! Two more ahead, closing in, trying to cut us off.

<Don't fight them, keep moving!>

But two lines were converging: two Venber, six bears, with the hangar side-door being the point of intersection.

WHUMPF!

The first Venber hit Jake headlong. Jake missed the door and slammed hard against the side of the hangar. He left a big dent in the corrugated metal.

Tobias, right behind him, lunged for the Venber, roaring.

The Venber swung one of his beefy twin arms and knocked Tobias sprawling. He might as well have been a teddy bear.

A second Venber was closing on me. If I fought, I'd lose. Keep running! STOP! I dug in my claws. A shower of ice crystals and the Venber blew past me, too clumsy to turn in time.

The monster crashed headlong into the side of the hangar. Now we didn't need a door. There was a nice, big, Bugs-Bunny-runs-through-the-door kind of hole. You could almost make out the Venber's silhouette in the steel.

Cassie ploughed into me, knocking me forward. We both picked ourselves up and hauled.

The first Venber was after Jake, swinging arms that would shatter Jake's bones if they connected.

<Don't worry about me! GO!> Jake said, seeing us hesitate.

We went. Tobias was already picking himself up to give Jake a hand, so we went. Through the hole. Into . . . warmth!

Bright lights! A huge space. Two parked Bug fighters!

And there, on the floor between us and the nearest Bug fighter, a Venber.

Or what was left of him.

Chapter 26

Silent, ghastly, he writhed. The lower half of his body was already a spreading pool of viscous liquid. A powerful smell hit us. Like chlorine or something.

The top half of the Venber kept reaching for us. Trying to obey its programming. It was nothing but a biological computer. A hideous creation of the Yeerks. Even in its own death throes it could do nothing but obey its programming.

We splashed through the Venber's liquid body. There was no other way. I felt a chemical tingle on my paws. I tracked it on to the floor beyond.

<Jake!> I yelled. <Get them into the hangar!>

Human-controllers now, rushing around from behind the Bug fighter. Dracon beams in their hands, but they were too slow.

"Hhhhhrrroooohhhwwwr!"

Rachel and Ax roared and ploughed into them. The human-Controllers went down like bowling pins.

Jake and Tobias came up behind, still running, bloodied, their white fur ripped away in chunks. Two big Venber were after them.

The two Venber hit the warm air. They kept charging, even as their ski feet turned to glue.

Another, right behind them. Charging, deadly one second, then pitiful the next.

I froze there, staring. Watching the mindless suicide. They came at us, leaping through the gap, slowing, stumbling, falling, melting.

Ax was aboard the nearest Bug fighter. I snapped out of my horrified trance and realized they all were. All but Cassie and I.

We waited till all eight of the Venber at the base had destroyed themselves. I don't know why. With all the danger, all the terror, someone still needed to be a witness. Someone needed to be able to tell the world someday about this Yeerk atrocity.

<Marco! Cassie! What are you doing? Come on!> Rachel yelled.

We turned away, with Venber remains staining our footsteps, and crammed aboard the

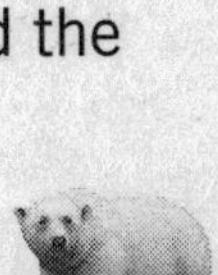

Bug fighter. The others were already demorphing. Otherwise there'd be no way to fit this much bear into a ship designed for a Hork-Bajir, a Taxxon, and maybe one or two passengers.

Ax was emerging from the bear, blue fur replacing white, his stalk eyes rising from the bear's quizzical brow. His paws were slimming down into Andalite fingers as he engaged the ship's controls.

<We are powered up, Prince Jake,> Ax said calmly. <Who will take weapons?>

<I will,> I said.

The Bug fighter rose gently from the hangar floor. Through the transparent forward panels we could see human-Controllers splashing through the almost entirely liquefied Venber. One Venber head and arm were still . . . and then that was gone, too.

I was more human than bear. I'd been aboard a Bug fighter before, and I more or less knew the weapons station. Not much to it, really. Easier than a Nintendo joystick.

"The other Bug fighter," Jake said, sounding very calm.

Ax turned our ship till our two Dracon spikes were aimed point-blank at the other ship.

<Low power, please,> Ax suggested.

I fired. Even at low power the concussion from the disintegrating Bug fighter knocked us back against one of the corrugated steel walls.

We swivelled and blew the wall into atoms. Ax kicked the ship into gear and we were out in the night, circling above the base.

"The dish," Jake said.

I fired.

TSEEEEEEW!

The dish blew into atoms.

"That building over there."

TSEEEEEEW! Building gone.

We systematically destroyed the base, building by building, vehicle by vehicle. Each time, we allowed time for the human-Controllers to run like scared sheep. It was the base we wanted, not them.

Finally, Jake said, "The hangar."

I aimed and fired. The last remains of the Venber became smoke and steam and loose atoms.

"Rest in peace," someone said. It turned out to be Rachel.

We hauled up and out and south as fast as the little ship would move. But we didn't get far.

<Sensor probe!> Ax yelled. His hands flew over the console. <We're being probed by. . .> He waited while the ship's computer came up with the answer.

<The Blade ship, Prince Jake. It is on an intercept course.>

"Can we outrun it? Lose it?"

<No. However, we can travel some distance before it catches us.>

We raced south. The Blade ship came on like a cheetah after a pig. We had a big head-start, but the cheetah was going to be enjoying bacon, and nothing was going to change that.

Three minutes before the Blade ship would have intercepted us, we blew the Bug fighter to smithereens. It was a huge fireball in someone's night sky. No doubt a lot of people saw it and wondered.

They did not see the six birds of prey that floated down to Earth.

Chapter 27

It took two more days for us to get home. We hid out on trains and trucks. We flew. We enjoyed the warmth.

Once, as we floated high on a wonderful warm thermal, we talked about the Venber. There were still two who might be alive, wandering the frozen Arctic. They might even know that the creatures they'd chased were human. A loose end. But the Venber wouldn't be heading south to civilization any time soon.

<Next time you hear a story about an Abominable Snowman, maybe there'll be some truth to it,> Tobias pointed out.

Don't know why we cared. The Venber had tried to kill us. Only *they* hadn't tried to do anything. They were helpless tools of the Yeerks.

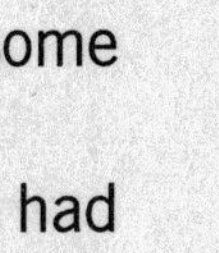

Victims of a long-ago tragedy, brought back to life only to write a new chapter of cruelty.

We made it home and relieved the Chee who'd taken our places. I don't know if they were glad to be done playing their parts or not. Who can tell what an android thinks?

I put the whole thing behind me. You have to do that. You can't be in a war and think about all the stuff that happens. You can't keep all the fear and all the pain right there in the front part of your brain, you know? You go nuts like that.

But some things are hard to get past. Sometimes it's the little things.

"Marco? Are you still alive?" my dad yelled up the stairs.

"Yeah, Dad," I answered.

"You've been in there for an hour! Are you ever coming out?"

"Well, sure, eventually," I said.

"Could you at least turn on the fan? The whole house is turning into a sauna."

"Sorry," I said. "I forgot."

That was a lie. I hadn't forgotten. I *wanted* the whole house to feel like a sauna. And I was considering staying in the shower for ever.

Heat. Man, heat is a very, very nice thing. For humans, anyway.

"Marco!" My dad, yelling again, this time from somewhere closer by.

"What?" I yelled back through the steam.

"Your room is a total pigsty!"

When I'd got home, I'd been horrified to see *someone* had cleaned my room. I mean, cleaned it. There was not a crisp packet to be found! So much for Erek playing the role of me. Hah!

"I suppose I shouldn't have expected this sudden neat stage to last," my dad muttered outside the bathroom door.

"Yeah, well," I said, reluctantly turning off the tap.

"I appreciate what you did to the basement and garage, though. I've never seen them look so good."

"Oh, sure," I replied. "Say, did Marian happen to call in the last couple of days?"

"In the last couple of days?" Dad repeated. "No. I would have told you if she had."

"Oh," I said. "Oh, well."

"Hey, you want to go out and catch something to eat?"

I stuck my wet head out of the door. "Like what?"

"I was thinking ice-cream."

"Ice-cream."

"Yeah. Ice-cream."

"Excuse me." I closed the door, stepped back in the shower, and turned on the water. Hot. Very, very hot.

Don't miss

ANIMORPHS®

26 The Attack

Crayak turned his blood-red eye on me, watching as I lay helpless. Watching as the Howlers stood around Cassie in a circle, watching as they lowered their claw hands into place, watching and laughing as she stood, eyes closed, helpless, seconds away from—

"Cassie! Look out!"

I jerked up, eyes wide, hands flailing, fending off an attack.

"Chill, chill," Marco said. He grabbed one hand and Rachel grabbed the other. "It's OK, dude, fight's over."

I looked around, still wild. A room. Walls of solid colours, one red, the others yellow. Still in Lego Land.

I slapped my legs. Human. My arms. Human. All me, with no ragged holes.

I'd made it out of morph. I looked round the room. Rachel and Marco. Tobias sitting on the back of a strangely shaped chair. Erek standing alone, head down in thought. Ax as far from me as he could get, all four eyes turned away.

"Cassie?" I asked.

"I'm here," she said. I realized she was behind me. I felt her palm on my cheek. Then she put her arms around me and hugged me from behind. It made me want to cry.

"It's taken you a while to wake up," Cassie said. "You barely demorphed in time. Then it was like you were in a coma, like you weren't going to wake up at all."

I remembered dreams. They were dreams, weren't they? Hard to be sure. Reality itself was weird enough to be a dream.

"The Howler?" I asked Rachel.

Her mouth was an angry line. "We hurt him. But he walked away."

"Six against one and we got a draw," Marco said angrily.

"Not six," Rachel corrected. "Seven. Erek saved our butts. He was the only one who could handle the howls."

"Yeah, right, thanks a huge load, Erek," Marco said angrily. "He gave us directions. Not to hurt the Howler, you understand, 'cause that would violate his programming. But directions on how to crawl out of there."

I held on to Cassie's hand. I didn't want to get into this. I wanted to hold on to a moment of feeling glad to be alive, glad to feel Cassie's concern.

Then I sighed, squeezed her fingers, and pushed her hand away. "Erek did what he could, Marco. You know that as well as I do. My brain was scrambled. I'd be dead without him. That's enough for me."

Marco looked like he wanted to say something else, but then his anger collapsed. "Yeah. We all did what we could."

I spotted Guide back against a wall, uncharacteristically quiet. "You stick with us after that?" I asked him.

His eyes glowed. <Oh, yes, yes, yes. I will be able to sell the memory of that battle for a small fortune! And if each of you would sell me your own unique perspectives, I could buy my own corner with the profits!>

I drew Cassie around to where I could see her. I nodded at Ax. "What's with him?" I asked.

She shook her head. "He ran away. He came back, but I suppose that's not enough. He won't talk to anyone."

"Let him be for a while," I said. "Then I'll talk to him."

I felt weary. Bruised and beaten, although

my human body reconstructed from DNA was unscarred by the battle. It was my brain that was worn out. I could see similar feelings on the faces around me.

We'd been beaten in a fair fight. No, not a fair fight. It had been six of us plus Erek against one Howler. We'd fought to a draw. A tie. Seven against one. A tie.

If there had been two Howlers, let alone all seven, we'd have been killed in ten seconds.

We weren't scared, not the way we might be, facing a battle. We were worse than scared: we were beaten.

"What is this place?" I asked.

Rachel shrugged. "Some place Guide got for us. This room and a bathroom — well, I think it's a bathroom. Hope it's a bathroom."

A pile of rags lay in one corner. Our clothing. What was left of it after we'd morphed while still wearing it. We were in our morphing outfits now. But I guessed we didn't look any more out of place than we would have, anyway. The Iskoort probably didn't care much about human fashion.

<What do we do?> Tobias asked.

"I'm for dialling up the Ellimist and telling him to go jump off whatever super-dimensional bridge he can find," Marco said.

<He wouldn't have put us here if we weren't at least theoretically capable of winning,> Tobias said.

"Unless there's some other, deeper game the Ellimist is playing," Cassie said. "He's fighting a battle for entire species, entire planets. We're just pawns."

That was more cynicism than I was used to hearing from Cassie. But she wasn't wrong. The Ellimist and Crayak were both way over our heads. And I was haunted by the suggestion that maybe this was all a set-up. That maybe Crayak wanted us here. Not because we were important by ourselves, but because eliminating us would help the Yeerks.

Why had the Ellimist brought us here? He had to know how powerful the Howlers were. Had to.

"This is a rotten, stinking deal," Rachel said, expressing the thoughts in my own head. "We're leaving our own planet defenceless to save these Iskoort." She said "Iskoort" like a curse word.

I found myself looking at Erek. I could only imagine what was going on inside his head. He had the power to fight Howlers and win. But wasn't able to fight.

Erek said, "Maybe the Ellimist would re-program me. Remove the prohibition against violence."

Marco groaned. "Well, it's official: the situation is hopeless. When Erek starts talking that way it's because we're beaten."

"Beat *this*," Rachel said rudely.

It made me smile. Rachel felt as down as anyone, but she refused to admit she couldn't just go out and nail the next Howler she saw.

"They're faster than we are, stronger than we are, better armed than we are," Cassie said glumly. Then she lifted her face, eyes wary. "But are they smarter than we are?"

"Erek?" I asked him.

He sighed, a very human reaction. "They had faster-than-light ships at a time when humans still thought the wheel was a radical new invention."

<Doesn't make them smarter,> Tobias said. <The Ellimist said some species evolve quickly, others slowly. If you get a billion years' head start, of course you have better weapons and technology than a species that started later. Doesn't mean you're smarter. Maybe it just means you started earlier.>

It was a weak thread to hang by. But it was all we had.

"Erek? Tell us all you know about the Howlers," I said.

Creatures

The Series With Bite!

Everyone loves animals. The birds in the trees. The dogs running in the park. That cute little kitten.

But don't get too close. Not until you're sure. Are they ordinary animals – or are they creatures?

1. Once I Caught a Fish Alive
Paul's special new fish is causing problems. He wants to get rid of it, but the fish has other ideas...

2. If You Go Down to the Woods
Alex is having serious problems with the school play costumes. Did that fur coat just move?

3. See How They Run
Jon's next-door neighbour is very weird. In fact, Jon isn't sure that Frankie is completely human...

4. Who's Been Sitting in My Chair?
Rhoda's cat Opal seems to be terrified ... of a chair! But then this chair belongs to a very strange cat...

Look out for these new creatures...

5. Atishoo! Atishoo! All Fall Down!
Chocky the mynah bird is a great school pet. But now he's turning nasty. And you'd better do what he says...

6. Give a Dog a Bone
A statue of a faithful dog sounds really cute. But this dog is faithful unto death. And beyond...

Creatures – you have been warned!